# Liffey Rivers And The Mystery Of The Sparkling Solo Dress Crown

To order additional copies, please contact us.
BookSurge, LLC
www.booksurge.com
1-866-308-6235
orders@booksurge.com

BRENNA
BRIGGS

# LIFFEY RIVERS AND THE MYSTERY OF THE SPARKLING SOLO DRESS CROWN

2005

Liffey Rivers And The Mystery
Of The Sparkling Solo Dress
Crown

# TABLE OF CONTENTS

Chapter One: Checking In                                  1
Chapter Two: The Gateway                                  9
Chapter Three: The Skunk Man                             15
Chapter Four: A Crown                                    21
Chapter Five: In Harm's Way                              29
Chapter Six: Ignored                                     37
Chapter Seven: Lilacs                                    43
Chapter Eight: A Feis Father                             45
Chapter Nine: Aunt Cheerleader                           49
Chapter Ten: Suiting Up                                  53
Chapter Eleven: To Jig or Not to Jig                     63
Chapter Twelve: The Return of the Skunk Man              69
Chapter Thirteen: Down but Not Out                       73
Chapter Fourteen: Diamonds                               77
Chapter Fifteen: The Redheaded Woman                     83
Chapter Sixteen: Running                                 87
Chapter Seventeen: Collapse                              95
Chapter Eighteen: The Smell of a Skunk                   97
Chapter Nineteen: The Thinking Cap                      101
Chapter Twenty: Lost in the Fog                         105
Chapter Twenty-One: Chasing the Crown                   109
Chapter Twenty-Two: Conflict Diamonds                   113
Chapter Twenty-Three: The Messipi                       117
Chapter Twenty-Four:  Results                           121
Liffey's Lingo                                          127
Feis Cheers                                             133

*For All Those On The Quest For The Dress.*

# CHAPTER ONE
## Checking In

Liffey knew they were looking at her again. They always did when she arrived at the hotels. No one ever made direct eye contact with her, but she could *feel* them watching her as she checked in at the front desk...little clusters of dancers pretending to be stretching, as she passed by them on her way to the elevators that took forever to come.

She could see them in the lobby mirrors in back of her, pointing and whispering about "that girl with the name of that river in Ireland." If anyone ever *did* actually speak to her, they usually called her "Shannon," because that was the only name of a river in Ireland anyone seemed to know.

Liffey tossed her shoulder-length, light brown hair to the left and reached for the signing-in paperwork and pen that the desk clerk had pushed under her chin. Last year, the first time Liffey had gone through this routine, she had asked the clerk if she should sign her name in cursive. The pitying *"duh"* look she received had answered her question.

She would not make that mistake again. Confidently, Liffey picked up the pen and smoothly connected the letters of her name. Then she adjusted her backpack straps, turned, and strode purposefully past the huge

## CELTIC ARCH FEIS WELCOMES IRISH DANCERS!

banner into the crowd waiting for the elevators that always took at least ten minutes to get to the lobby on check-in day.

Always.

No matter *which* hotel.

No matter *how* many elevators there were.

It *always* took at least ten minutes of waiting and watching before the doors would finally open and take her up to her room. By the elevators, there were usually a few mothers staring at her and having a little chat among themselves with raised eyebrows, trying not to be noticed.

But Liffey *did* notice. Liffey noticed most things. Even the little things that most people just walked right by. She knew what the lobby mothers were thinking and talking about. Here she was again.

All alone.

Without a parent.

Or anyone for that matter.

*And she was only thirteen-years-old!*

Liffey resisted the urge to growl. She would save the growl for the twins if they turned up tomorrow.

*\*\*\**

Liffey wondered if the twins even knew how many trophies and medals they had won by now. They had probably stopped counting years ago.

At her Tuesday night dance class, she would often see the

twins coming out of their advanced classes as she was going into her beginner class. The only time one of the twins had ever even *looked* at Liffey and had actually spoken to her, was two years ago when Liffey was nervously standing back stage waiting to make her first entrance in her first ever St. Patrick's Day show. She was never really sure which one of them it was, but one of the twins came rushing off stage and rudely shoved her out of the way shouting *"move!"* like Liffey didn't matter at all.

To make sure a twin would not shove her out of their way *ever* again, Liffey often growled at one or both of them when they would accidentally pass by her and enjoyed watching them quickly change their direction if they spotted her first.

***

The ornate glass elevator cage finally arrived. Liffey was ready for it. She opened her large blue eyes wide and put on what she liked to think of as her cover girl smile, displaying her nearly perfect white teeth which were no longer hiding under rows of purple and pink braces. The smile was directed at the mothers who were hauling their daughters' dance bags and awkward dress carriers.

Feis arrival elevator rides always caused Liffey a great deal of anxiety because she was *sure* there was a solo dress in *every* dress carrier she watched being loaded on to *every* elevator at *every* feis she attended. She strongly suspected that *every* other Irish dancer in the whole entire *world* already *had* a solo dress. The fact that not one of those dresses belonged to her was a constant source of aggravation for Liffey.

Liffey sighed, forgetting her cover girl smile for the moment. She feared she would never get one of those lovely dresses. She *had* to get a first place in one of her Novice solo steps tomorrow so she would finally qualify for her own solo dress. And the only way to do that was to keep trying, so she put the smile back on her face and decided to leave her self-pity behind in the lobby.

\*\*\*

The elevator bell announced the doors were about to close.

Trying not to bump into the other passengers with her back pack, suitcase and bulky school dress carrier, Liffey clumsily elbowed her way into the crowded elevator.

Then she saw him.

Just as the elevator doors began to close, she saw *the man* in the marching band uniform step up and push his way on, sticking his leg in between the doors to hold them open until he could cram himself in.

There was some grumbling among the polite Irish dancers and their parents who were already *stuffed* into this elevator, but he cheerfully pushed through them and positioned himself directly behind Liffey. She pretended not to notice him. She had *really* hoped that this time she had slipped through unnoticed. Maybe he was not looking for her. "I'll just keep looking down and he might go away," thought Liffey. But she knew they *never* did.

Liffey's eyes were glued to the floor when she felt a light tap on her right shoulder and heard a deep voice say, "Excuse me, Miss Rivers," shifting Liffey's luggage from her hands into his. "I am your concierge, and I have orders to accompany you to your room." Liffey cringed, blushing bright red. He *knew* who she was! "How do they *always* know what I look like?"

Liffey shook her hair over her face, trying to mask her embarrassment at this uninvited intrusion. After counting to ten, she came out from under her hair tent and flashed a cover girl smile again at the large group of elevator riders who could no longer hide their curiosity, and were now openly staring at Liffey and her concierge.

After the bag exchange, the concierge stiffened his shoulders and positioned himself like a palace guard directly behind Liffey. He looked straight ahead with a no-nonsense stare. "He acts like a movie star bodyguard," Liffey mumbled. The badge he wore said his name was "Bert," like in Bert and Ernie. "Where are his *shades?*" Liffey scowled, realizing she was trapped.

Everyone still waiting for the other three elevators in the lobby below had seen Bert's interception of Liffey. They were openly gawking now, their necks stretching up like a bunch of geese, as they watched Liffey and the concierge in the glass elevator cage begin its slow ascent to the unknown floors above them.

\*\*\*

Whenever Liffey Rivers went to an Irish dance competition, she knew that her father, Robert Rivers, always paid extra at the feis hotel for her to be accompanied to and from her room by hotel staff. Liffey *hated* this, but her father insisted, and by now she was used to the routine although she always did her best to avoid it.

"Hotels are not legally allowed to have minors, let alone thirteen-year-olds, staying in their rooms without an adult," he patiently explained many times when Liffey *begged* him not to hire a man in a band uniform to grab her bags and push to the front of the crowds waiting for the elevators.

Liffey did not know how her father organized all this, but she knew his law firm in Chicago was paid a lot of money to arrange things in people's lives. She thought she had dodged this one though, because *this* time, she got as far as the elevators before she was snagged by "Bert the Bodyguard."

***

Liffey looked over her shoulder and managed a feeble smile for Bert, trying to hide her exasperation. She did not need this! She wondered how much her father had paid him to walk her to her room.

The elevator moved so slowly that Liffey could see the veins in the extended necks of the curious feis mothers in the lobby below. Someday she would have pamphlets printed and hand them out in hotel feis lobbies to the pointing girls and their nosy mothers.

She would call the pamphlet: *Stare At Your Own Risk.*

*That* might clue them in, and maybe then they would stare at their *feet* on the elevators instead of her.

Liffey deliberately tried to make the other elevator passengers feel as uncomfortable as she did. She kept the cover girl smile on her face for the entire ride up to the 5th floor, smiling at everyone the whole time and making everyone very nervous. The concierge shrugged his shoulders at the other passengers as if to say he had *no* idea why Liffey was behaving in this curious manner.

Every few seconds, Liffey would exhale loudly through her teeth and then make another loud sucking-in-air noise. Bert politely pretended not to notice the rude noises she was making, while the other elevator passengers' eyes shifted uncomfortably to their feet. "Where they should have been in the first place," thought Liffey.

Liffey Rivers and the concierge got off the elevator on the 5th floor. Liffey immediately sprang into her hop 1-2-3s. She was already half way down the hall in front of Bert by the time he picked up her bags and began padding down the corridor behind her to Room 503.

Still wearing the frozen smile from the elevator and hissing through her clenched teeth, Liffey stood at the door to her room and waited for Bert. Her jaw was beginning to hurt. As she watched poor Bert scrambling down the hallway, she wondered how many rooms on this floor were reserved by dancers and their families for tomorrow's feis.

The concierge finally made it and opened the door. He placed her bags in the spacious hallway leading into the bedroom, told Liffey how nice it was to have met her, handed her another room key and fled. Peering into the hallway after him, Liffey kept the grimace on her face until Bert was out of sight. Then she closed the door with a sigh of relief and slowly relaxed her clenched facial muscles.

# CHAPTER TWO
## The Gateway

Delighted to be alone at last, Liffey ran to the windows and pulled open the heavy beige drapes, thinking how much she liked this Celtic Arch Feis. She had been to it last year, and her father must have remembered how much she loved this room with its great view of the Mississippi River, because he had reserved it for her again.

Opening the sliding door to the balcony, Liffey winced a little from a blast of wind that hit her in the face. She could see that a thunder storm was quickly forming and prematurely darkening the sky above her. The view was spectacular.

There it was! The famous "Gateway to the West." The St. Louis Arch! It looked like a huge magnet. She had studied the Arch in her 4th grade geography class.

Closing the door to get out of the rain that was now pouring over her balcony like a waterfall, Liffey tried to picture brave pioneers in their wagon trains crossing over the "Father of

Waters," the Native American name for the Mississippi River winding along below her.

The River reminded Liffey of her 3rd grade teacher's love for Native American culture. Mrs. Hankins had tried to explain to the class the injustice of taking away land that did not belong to you, like the land the pioneers settled on, *after* they took it away from the Indians who had already been there for thousands of years. "Then, after the settlers *took* the land," said Mrs. Hankins, "everybody called it progress." Nobody but Liffey seemed to get her point.

What would it be like now, Liffey wondered looking down at the crowded city below her, if the wagon trains had never crossed the "Messipi" (Mrs. Hankins had drilled that word into them), and the Father of Waters was not brown and dirty from pollution. One thing *was* certain. If none of that had happened, Liffey knew she would not be standing here now looking at the Arch.

The cloudburst stopped as quickly as it had started.

The Arch was now reflecting the night lights of downtown St. Louis. Liffey remembered how last summer it had a golden glow right at sunset, just before dark. She wished she had checked in earlier today and made a mental note not to miss the "glow show" if she came back to this feis again next year.

Liffey was staring so intensely at the glowing Arch that her eyes began to go out of focus, so she crossed her eyes to double it. Now there were two of them! Just as Liffey was trying to *triple* cross her eyes and see if she could make three Arches, she felt herself slipping into a solo dress trance.

*** 

There it was! She could see it clearly. A totally *incredible*, one-of-a-kind solo dress crown!

It was an *exact replica* of the St. Louis Arch! Remembering her geography facts, she knew the Arch was made out of concrete and stainless steel. "So it would reflect light," Liffey reasoned scientifically. She would construct a tiny steel replica Arch using heavy file fasteners from her father's office. She would light the Arch crown from different angles, hiding little lights throughout her wig. Then maybe the adjudicators would be so interested in her unusual crown, they might not notice her sloppily turned out feet!

"I *really* need to work on my turn out," Liffey fretted, slowly coming out of the solo dress daze.

Next, Liffey plotted how she might take the St. Louis Arch *down* after the feis was over and move it to a different spot. Like maybe her backyard in Wisconsin. Or maybe further up the Mississippi River, about a five hour drive from her house to a cliff where hundreds of bald eagles nested. She would place the Arch in between the rocky bluffs where the birds lived. At dawn, she would watch the birds coasting along on invisible air streams, soaring over and under the Arch like the current of the Father of Rivers below it.

*** 

Liffey thought these thoughts as she picked up the room phone on the table by the bed. It was time to order the pre-feis spaghetti and meatballs.

Liffey *always* ate spaghetti and meatballs the night before a feis, no matter *where* she was. No matter *what* time it was. She *had* to eat spaghetti and meatballs or she might jinx the feis the next day. Her father would say that this was obsessive compulsive behavior if he ever figured out that the *real* reason Liffey insisted on preparing dinner herself the night before a feis (if it was close to home), was to make absolutely *certain* that it *was* spaghetti and meatballs. She knew she could not take *any* chances of someone else serving a roast, or other non-spaghetti-and-meatball-dinner, the night before a feis.

\*\*\*

Liffey remembered from last year that the meatballs here in St. Louis were good, but the *best* meatballs she had ever eaten in her *life* were in Boston at a neighborhood family restaurant where she had dined with her father. They were the size of her father's *fist*.

Those meatballs were so amazing that Liffey had asked her father after dinner if they could move to Boston so she could eat them every day. He pretended to seriously consider the idea, but then broke out laughing and said that he did not think he could relocate his fifty-person law practice all the way to Massachusetts just so his daughter could eat big meatballs every day. Still, Liffey was certain that if her father's staff could just *taste* those meatballs, they would be only too happy to relocate to Boston.

\*\*\*

When the average-sized St. Louis meatballs and pasta arrived, Liffey ate them quickly because she wanted to power-walk around the hotel lobby which was probably crowded with dancers by now. She needed to see if there was anyone at this feis she recognized. Not that it would matter much, but then somebody other than herself might notice if she won a medal the next day.

Since Liffey had not yet signed in at the feis registration desk, she could not look up the names of the competitors who would be alphabetically listed in the feis welcome booklet. It was more fun anyway to power-walk around the lobby to see if anyone looked familiar.

And there was always the hope of a twin sighting!

Before Liffey finished lacing up her ghillies and getting ready for the lobby-walking, she remembered to call the front desk and ask for an escort as her father insisted she do each time she was coming to or going from her hotel room. Liffey hated doing this, but she tried to obey her father because she knew that he would not ask her to do this unless he thought it was very important.

When she heard the loud knock at the door, she looked through the little peephole to make sure it was Bert. It was, so she opened the door and leapt right into the hall past the startled concierge. She could hear him thumping along the hall behind her as she did her hop 1-2-3 skipping steps down the long corridor on the way to the elevators.

They were alone on the elevator, so Liffey decided to make small talk with Bert. She asked him very sincerely if he wanted to meet her imaginary dancer friend who happened to be riding down on the elevator with them. His beady little eyes darted around uncomfortably looking for Liffey's invisible friend. Bert finally said that it would indeed be nice to meet the imaginary friend, and asked Liffey what her name was.

"Her name is 'Feshanna'" Liffey replied very seriously as the elevator arrived at the lobby level.

Bert clearly did not get the joke, so Liffey tried another one, and asked him if he would please take "Feshanna" back up to the room while she warmed up for tomorrow's feis. Bert nodded, looking uneasily at the crowd waiting to get on their elevator.

"Oh—and would you please talk to her on the way up so she doesn't look down and freak out?" requested Liffey, now standing outside the elevator with the next group waiting to get on.

Then Liffey watched as the concierge, who was trying very hard not to be noticed, shuffled to the back of the elevator. He turned sideways, cupped his right hand over his face and began talking into the panel of elevator glass.

Bert very much hoped that the other elevator passengers were talking among themselves and would not notice his conversation with Miss Rivers' imaginary friend.

*This* time, *Liffey* was the one stretching her neck like a goose as she watched a grownup man talking to himself in a glass elevator! She gave Bert a little wave of encouragement as the elevator went out of people-sighting range.

# CHAPTER THREE
## The Skunk Man

Liffey liked to power-walk around a hotel to work off her pre-feis spaghetti and meatball dinners. But tonight, right as she got into her stride, she stopped dead in her tracks.

There, directly in front of her, checking in at the front desk in the hotel lobby was *that man* again! She had seen him at other competitions. Liffey remembered him because he had a streak of white hair, like a skunk, running straight down the middle of the back of his head. His hair was black otherwise and cut short with a kind of spiked up look. He seemed to be always alone like her. She didn't think he was a vendor because Liffey knew most of the Midwest feis vendors by sight. Yet she had seen this man several times before.

Liffey could not remember what, if anything, she had ever seen him *do* at the other competitions, but he did not seem to be a spectator. And he certainly looked *nothing* like a parent! He had a bored look about him. Kind of like one of the non-dancer brothers or sisters who were obviously dragged to Irish dance competitions on a forced family trip and expected to watch their sisters or brothers compete all day. However, she never *saw* him with any of the dancers, or anyone else for that matter. He was always alone. She had nicknamed him the "skunk man" the second time she had seen him at a feis.

The skunk man finished checking in and walked over

to the elevators. He looked preoccupied and distracted as he stared at the unopened elevator doors.

Liffey merged into the elevator crowd to get a closer look at him. *This* time, she kept her mouth *shut* and tried to blend in. She was curious about this man who seemed to be so often *at* a feis but never *part* of one. She decided to follow him onto the elevator in case he said or did something that might explain what he was doing here. Liffey stretched and pointed her toes and looked at her wristwatch like she actually had somewhere to go and someone to meet.

When the elevator doors on her right finally opened, she quietly slipped in behind the skunk man with a few other dancers and their parents. She was relieved to see that there was no one on the elevator that she recognized who might start whispering about her and cause the skunk man to notice her. The skunk man pressed 6. The others pressed 8. Liffey heard herself say: "I'm going to the eighth floor too."

***

Liffey thought that one of the *few* benefits of not having any friends, and coming to Irish dance competitions without any family, was that you could pretty much do *what* you wanted to do *when* you wanted to do it! She was sure that many of life's adventures never happened for most girls her age because they always had to ask permission to do something, and by the time it took to get the permission, the moment was gone!

Like the time she was riding the down escalator at a New York City department store. There, directly across from her, going up the up escalator, was Jeremy Knife *in person*!

Liffey sensed right away that this was a *once* in a lifetime opportunity, so she immediately ran down the moving escalator stairs, turned sharply trying not to knock any nice old ladies down, and scrambled on to the up escalator, brushing past the other riders as carefully as she could.

She noticed that a few other frantic girls had also recognized him as she ran by them on the landing. They were *begging* their mothers for permission to follow him. But it was too late for them because before she ever saw if they even got their permission, she and Jeremy Knife made a sharp right turn at the top of the escalator stairs and walked quickly into the toy department *together*!

Sort of.

After all, she *had* walked into the room with him!

Liffey was somewhat surprised to see this huge celebrity walking into the toy department. She positioned herself directly in back of him, pretending not to know who he was, and trying very hard to look casual, like she was actually shopping. She could see that he was studying a table piled high with plush jungle animals.

*Then* magically, he *smiled* at her and *then* he actually *spoke* to her in his polished British accent: "Excuse me, I need some advice here. You're a girl." (He had *noticed* she was a girl!) Liffey tried not to shriek out something stupid like "*I know*! *I know*!"

"Would you mind helping me out here? Which one of these stuffed creatures do you think an eight-year-old girl might fancy?"

Liffey's heart sank. How *old was* he anyway? *Surely* he did not have an eight-year-old daughter at home who called him "Daddy!"

Trying to keep her composure, Liffey managed to answer his question. "Sure, I'd be happy to help out. You're Jeremy Knife, aren't you?"

He replied that he was, and together they picked out a life-sized baby tiger, for who turned out to be his little *sister*! Liffey made sure to let "Jeremy" know she was *much* older than his younger sibling. "I am twelve. Actually, I'm almost thirteen," she informed him. Liffey wanted to add that she would wait for him forever as well, but flashed him her cover girl smile instead.

He seemed genuinely grateful for her help, as he reached into a jacket pocket and pulled out his latest CD. He wrote on it: "To Liffey Rivers, with many thanks for her expert advice and good taste. Cheers, Jeremy Knife."

"*That* was the kind of adventure you could have if you didn't have to always back track and get permission," thought Liffey.

\*\*\*

Liffey was not sure yet what kind of adventure was connected with the skunk man. But there was one. She could *feel* it!

As the elevator climbed slowly upward, Liffey began to carefully study the skunk man as quickly as she could without drawing attention to herself. If the two remaining dancers and their parents got off the elevator *before* the skunk man did, even though they had pressed the 8 button and he had pressed 6, and nobody else got *on* the elevator, she would find herself alone with him. She knew she could not risk this because of her father's absolute rule that she *never* be alone on an elevator or in a hallway, or *anywhere* in a hotel, except her own room. Besides, being alone with the skunk man would be like being put into a reptile cage. He gave Liffey the creeps!

Liffey edged forward a little closer to the skunk man and saw that he was holding a shopping bag in his left hand. The bag was open, so she bent down and pretended to tie her right ghillie lace while she craned her neck a bit to try and see what was in it. She was surprised when she saw the curly wig, and then the body of a porcelain Irish dancer doll.

The doll was dressed in an Irish dancing school costume.

"Why on earth did the skunk man have an Irish dancer doll?" Liffey was puzzled. "He looks more like someone who would be carrying poker chips around in a shopping bag," thought Liffey, activating the detective lobe of her brain.

# CHAPTER FOUR
## A Crown

Liffey sensed that something was not quite right with this doll's attire. But she needed to get a better look at the doll to figure out what it was. She bent down again and this time pretended to tie her *left* ghillie, while she stretched her neck to get a better glimpse into the shopping bag.

The doll was not carefully wrapped with tissue paper like a fragile porcelain doll normally would be. It was just plopped inside the shopping bag. Liffey could see that the doll was wearing a green Irish dance school dress, embroidered with squiggly white Celtic circle designs. But something was very *wrong* with this doll.

Suddenly, Liffey *knew* what it was! Perched on top of the doll's brown curls was a *diamond solo dress crown* instead of a proper school dress headband. Liffey *knew* that an Irish dance school costume was *never* worn with a solo dress crown. Never ever!

\*\*\*

Liffey was so certain about this because she was somewhat of an expert on solo dresses and solo dress crowns. Her father often teased her about her obsession with getting her first solo dress. He called it her "quest for the dress."

Liffey had already sketched about a *hundred* solo dresses with every color and Irish symbol she could find or invent. She purchased dress designer computer software. She even created her own web page where she displayed the "Top 10" finalist dresses she had designed. As soon as she nabbed the first place, she would open up online voting for the dresses. The winner dress would then immediately be moved into production. She was *totally* ready for "Operation Solo Dress!"

Unfortunately, much of the knowledge that Liffey had collected about the solo dress world was due to the fact that nobody ever really talked to her at competitions. This meant she was able to listen to the conversations *other* people were having around her, if she could blend in and go unnoticed. And she usually could. She had discovered years ago that grownups did not seem to notice children unless they were their own.

Apparently, based on her eavesdropping, she learned that it could take a very long time to actually *get* a solo dress after it had been ordered. Like months and months. This drove mothers crazy and made their dancer daughters irritable and whiny.

Also, according to the information her spying gave her, it must be almost impossible to convince a dress maker that getting the dress they were making was actually a matter of *life or death* for the dancer and her mother.

This worried Liffey a great deal because she wanted to use a far away Dublin dress designer whose dresses she greatly admired on the dancers who were lucky enough to be wearing them. And since she did not even *have* a mother to make phone calls begging for *her* dress to be completed, and knowing how *totally* impatient she would be *waiting* for *her* dress, Liffey knew there was only one solution.

She would have to persuade her father to let her go to Ireland to stake out the dress maker's shop—just in case they did not know that *her* dress needed to be completed within *hours* of ordering it and that it really *was* a matter of life or death as far as *her* solo dress was concerned! Liffey feared she might literally explode with joy when "Operation Solo Dress" time actually arrived.

***

Liffey continued to analyze the doll. She was well aware that a solo dress *crown* was usually made by the dressmaker to *match* a solo *dress*. Every now and then, Liffey had seen a tiara being worn as a kind of special effect *with* a solo dress crown. However, she could not remember *ever* seeing a diamond crown being worn with an Irish dance *school* dress. Yet this doll was wearing an oversized crown with diamonds as big as marbles! And it was not a tasteful, princess-tiara-kind-of-crown.

The crown was obviously *much* too big for the little doll's head. Not only was the doll wearing an oversized crown, but the crown had *way* too many jewels on it. There were so many diamonds that it reminded Liffey of the Royal Crown Jewels she had seen on display at the Tower of London when she was ten-years-old.

***

When Liffey had toured the Tower, she rode the moving sidewalk over and over past the Royal Crown Jewels in their long glass cases. Liffey was so thrilled with the Tower's treasures that she made up her mind she would remain there forever. She schemed how she might be able to hide out and then spend the rest of her *life* just riding by the jewels all day long. Of course she would have to take breaks occasionally and look for food scraps that tourists would leave behind in the tea room restaurant. *And* she would have to find some place to sleep, which might prove to be difficult. But it *could* work! She would let her father know she was safe from time to time. Maybe she could train one of the Tower ravens to deliver messages like a carrier pigeon. Then she could send word that she was o.k. regularly to her father. She would miss him terribly, but the jewels were calling her! Her father would just have to understand.

Liffey's plan to ride by the jewels for the rest of her life on the moving sidewalk ended abruptly, however, when a guard quietly approached her after he had counted her 100th pass. Politely, but firmly, he said, "Young lady! You cannot ride by these Crown Jewels all day long! Where are your parents?"

*That* question frequently came up because Liffey often had no one with her in public. Liffey had become an expert at escaping from her sitters. She called her sitters "keepers," because they had a very difficult time *keeping* up with her!

Before Liffey's thirteenth birthday, the keeper of the day was supposed to stay with her at all times. Nonetheless, Liffey usually managed to get away from her keeper and hide—especially in museums and art galleries. Sooner or later, she was snared by an official of some sort and returned to the keeper. Then the keeper would tattle on her and *then* Liffey would be grounded for a week.

Because of this keeper-dodging pattern, Liffey had missed many feiseanna over the past two years, and many chances to work towards earning her solo dress.

After her thirteenth birthday, her father stopped the keeper system and Liffey was expected to act responsibly and to behave properly in public. He especially expected her to take elaborate safety precautions. Liffey had not yet let her father down. She was careful to watch everybody around her and had developed an instinct, or *feeling* for when something was dangerous or not quite right with a situation.

Liffey could not have guessed now riding in this elevator, that the instincts she had developed over the years of playfully dodging her sitters would save her life within the next twenty-four hours!

***

Liffey snapped out of her remembering trance and looked again at the crown on the doll. The diamonds looked so *real*! The doll's pretty porcelain face had almost no expression, but the diamonds on the crown were flashing like a fireworks display! They were *dazzling*! Liffey was absolutely *certain* that she had never seen a feis vendor selling Irish dancer dolls with solo dress crowns. And the few tiaras that she *had* seen were for dancers, not dolls.

The dolls usually wore a school costume and a headband of some sort. You simply could *not* mix a school dress with a solo dress crown. The same way you could not mix a school headband with a solo dress. Or loud rap music with a parent. Or peanut butter with raw eggs!

Liffey had almost decided to just go ahead and boldly ask the skunk man where he *got* the lovely doll, when pins and needles began running up and down her spine like an electric shock. Uncomfortable, prickly sensations. The last time Liffey had felt these sensations, she had narrowly missed being run over by a truck in the Loop! It was like an internal alarm system that would warn Liffey if *something* or *someone* dangerous was nearby.

Her head began to throb.

Then she felt them.

Eyes directed at her like two red laser beams.

Liffey had *forgotten* to keep tying her ghillie and was now *obviously* staring at the doll's diamond crown. Her right hand had begun to reach out, almost touching the doll's head, like Sleeping Beauty walking to prick the spinning wheel with her outstretched finger. Stopping her hand from touching the crown just in time, Liffey looked up slowly and flashed a weak smile at the skunk man. He continued to stare at her coldly. Liffey shivered a little.

Suddenly she was *sure* that the skunk man was up to something! Liffey hoped he did not know that she somehow knew this. She shivered again. The pins and needles felt like a live creature crawling up and down her back.

The elevator reached the 6th floor, and the skunk man walked stiffly out through the opening doors. Relieved to see him leaving, Liffey watched the back of his white striped head enter the hallway and turn left. She was confused and somewhat frightened when, instead of completing his turn, he pivoted around like a dancer and deliberately fixed two lifeless eyes upon her. Now Liffey positively *knew* that he *knew* that she *knew* something was not right!

Liffey tried to control her rising panic. She took a deep breath, put on her cover girl smile again and aimed it directly at the skunk man. He did not return the smile. His cloudy, hollow eyes remained fixed on Liffey, like a snake waiting for something to swallow, as the elevator doors slammed together. She had seen eyes like those before, but they had been in a nightmare.

Liffey *forced* herself not to be *so* afraid that she would do something stupid. Even though she was trembling all over, she made herself put her "thinking cap" back on her head. It was a survival game her father had taught her. If she ever panicked, Liffey was to imagine that she had dropped her thinking cap. She would then bend down, pick it up, and put it back on her head. This would enable her to think clearly again.

Thankfully, Liffey realized that the trick seemed to have worked this time. The paralyzing fear the skunk man's eyes had brought upon her was under control. She *could* think again!

\*\*\*

The fact that the skunk man had gotten off on the 6th floor and turned left interested Liffey a great deal because she knew that there were only very expensive suites on the left wing of the 6th floor. The left wing suites cost at least twenty times more than the regular rooms at this hotel.

Liffey only knew this because at last year's Celtic Arch Feis, she had actually tried to check herself into one of those expensive suites to "play movie star for the weekend," as she later told her disapproving father.

She was removed like baggage an hour after she had checked into the luxurious rooms. A concierge had come to her door and informed her that her father had telephoned the hotel to make sure his daughter had arrived safely. Robert Rivers had been informed that his daughter was in one of "those" suites and had not checked into the room that had been reserved for her.

Liffey had been politely transferred back down to the 5th floor and deposited in a regular room. When she had talked to her father later on that day, he told her he expected her to stay in a *real* room where *real* people stayed, and that neither she, nor anyone else on this planet, needed such ridiculous luxury.

\*\*\*

So, thought Liffey, coming back to the moment at hand, either the skunk man *has* a lot of money, or he was going to *see* someone who had a lot of money who was staying in one of those expensive suites.

Was he going there to give somebody the doll he was carrying around in that shopping bag?

"Wait a minute!" thought Liffey. "The feis vendors aren't even open yet! They don't start selling until tomorrow morning, right before the competitions begin. WHERE did he *get* that doll?"

That left turn made Liffey even more curious now about the skunk man and what he could be up to. He did not look or behave like someone who would be staying on the expensive 6th floor. That left hallway turn probably meant he was going to visit someone in one of those suites.

But who was that someone? And why did the skunk man turn up at so many feiseanna? Did he always have a doll with him? Liffey was going to find out!

# CHAPTER FIVE
## In Harm's Way

The elevator finally arrived at the 8th floor. Liffey held her finger on the door open button while the two remaining dancers and their parents noisily gathered up their luggage and got off the elevator.

Deep in thought about what her next move should be to solve the mystery of the sparkling solo dress crown, Liffey pressed the lobby button and the elevator bell signaled its impending descent. She wanted to get back to her power-walking and try to organize her thoughts again.

As the elevator doors swished shut, Liffey realized she was making a *big* mistake being on the down elevator alone. Even though the elevators were glass cages in some sections of this hotel, and she was riding in one of them now, her father insisted that she *never* be alone going to or from the lobby. She had already disobeyed him by following the skunk man onto this elevator to begin with. She wished now that she had never done it. But it was too late. She was in the elevator totally alone.

Within seconds, the creepy crawly sensations started up again, the tightening up and down her back with its prickly pins and needles. But this time, she felt like someone had just thrown a bucket of cold water over her head as well. Liffey's hide-and-seek instincts kicked in. She *knew* what she had to do. She *had* to get *off* this elevator!

Mechanically, Liffey watched as her right hand moved to the 7 button in a split second and pressed it fast enough so that the elevator actually stopped on the 7th floor. Then, still not knowing *why* she was doing it, Liffey jumped *off* the elevator and ducked down in the hallway next to the long fake ivy planter which served as a guardrail to the landing below. "What am I *doing*? Am I going *crazy*?" Liffey feared she might be having an out of body experience as she cowered, trying to figure out what in the world she was doing on the 7th floor landing.

The pins and needles were beginning to actually hurt now. She was grateful that there did not seem to be anyone walking along the hallway who might see her crouching by the plastic ivy planter. "It would be *just* my luck to have the twins see me now," thought Liffey, realizing she could not remain in that position for much longer without someone seeing her.

Liffey cautiously stood up and peered over the ledge.

Her absolute *worst* fear was *confirmed*! There was the skunk man, only one floor below, waiting to get back *on* the down elevator which she had just abandoned! He must have *guessed* she would be coming down again and that she had only been on the up elevator in the first place to snoop around in his business.

*Did* the skunk man think that Liffey was only *pretending* to be going up somewhere when she rode on the up elevator with him? If he *had* thought that, he was right!

Liffey needed to get back to the safety of the main lobby seven floors below. She peeked over the ledge again, far down to the lobby, and saw that there were crowds of dancers and musicians with their instruments waiting with their families by the elevators. This was one time Liffey wished she *did* have someone with her and that she *did* have to ask that someone's permission to do something!

Her heart was pounding as she tried to figure out what she needed to do now to avoid another encounter with the skunk man. Should she run down the exit stairs to the lobby? Her father had told her NEVER to be alone unless it was absolutely unavoidable. This *was* avoidable.

She could not risk getting back on another up or down elevator in case the skunk man was lurking around on one of the floors. After all, she had *just* seen the skunk man waiting at her down elevator! The skunk man would have been expecting Liffey to have been *on* that elevator *if* he thought she had been following him. That was probably why he was watching for her on the 6th floor landing! By now though, he would know that she was *not* on the down elevator and he might well be angry. Then what?

Liffey did not want to think about "then what."

She looked over the ivy again and saw that the skunk man had vanished! Did he ride the elevator back down to the lobby to look for her there when he saw she was not on it?

Unless...and this thought made Liffey turn to stone. *Unless*, when he had seen that Liffey was *not* on the down elevator, he did not get on the down elevator either and was now *hiding* in the stairwell listening, waiting for her to make a move to another floor!

"I am so dense!" moaned Liffey, realizing that if the skunk man *had* been watching the elevator lights, he would have seen the 8th floor light flash on and remain on as the slow moving dancers and their parents dragged their luggage off the elevator. Liffey had announced that *she* was headed for the 8th floor too. The skunk man would have heard her say that.

Then, *if* the skunk man were watching, he would have seen the 7th floor indicator light immediately blink on...the floor where Liffey really *had* gotten off the elevator! When the elevator reached the 6th floor it would have been *empty*. It was a dead give away that Liffey *had* gotten off the elevator on the 7th floor. An *empty elevator* had arrived at the 6th floor landing where the skunk man was waiting to confront Liffey because he suspected she had been following him.

What if the skunk man somehow *knew* she had gotten *off* on the 7th floor when he saw that she was not on the down elevator at the 6th floor level? "*Stupid* elevator lights," muttered Liffey, recognizing that the lights were a dead give away if someone who was up to no good was keeping an eye on them.

The skunk man was on a safari and the elevator lights were the tracks Liffey had left for him to hunt her down!

Liffey was now so frozen with fear she could not even do the thinking cap trick. It was apparent that she had to do *something* and she had to do it fast! There was *no way* she could risk going into the stairwell by herself. But she could not just keep crouching next to the ivy wall like some weirdo either. Anyone walking in the hallway would be able to see her there.

It suddenly dawned on Liffey that she had to actually *hide* now in case the skunk man was *walking* back up to this floor to look for her. Liffey had put herself in harm's way and had let herself and her father down. There was no turning back now.

Peering quickly down the long hallway, Liffey spotted a room service cart with an oversized white table cloth draped over it about fifty feet away from her. There did not seem to be anyone with the cart, so Liffey raced towards it and quickly hid herself under it. She was grateful to discover that the bottom shelf was empty and she did not have to lie down on top of someone's leftover food.

As she lay there motionless, feeling the cold steel on her legs, trying to breathe quietly, and wondering what in the *world* she should do next, the cart started with a jerk and began moving down the hall.

"Now what?" Liffey grumbled. Was she being *delivered* to a room? Or being taken back to the hotel kitchen? Liffey felt the cart stop. Then go. Then stop. Was someone trying to frighten her? Could the skunk man have seen her crawl under the cart and was *he* the one who was so roughly pushing and jerking the cart? Was he laughing to himself about how pathetic this poor little bimbo was? Stop again. Was a door opening? Should she try to roll off from under the cart and make a run for it?

Before she could make up her mind what the best plan of action would be, she was moving again, probably through a door because she felt a slight thud before stopping again.

Liffey could hear muffled voices inside and breathed easily again when she heard a friendly room service voice say: "Sorry! I was told to deliver this and just leave it inside the door. Somebody signed for it at the concierge desk. I didn't know anyone was in here."

"That's o.k.," a young girl's voice answered. "Just leave it, please.

"Yes, just leave me too!" thought Liffey, totally relieved she was not in the hands of the skunk man after all!

Liffey was out of harm's way for the moment but she knew she needed to regroup and plan her next move.

There did not seem to be any adults in the room as she listened to the voices discussing tomorrow's competition. The voices were going over the feis registration program trying to figure out who would be competing against them the next day.

"It's now or never," decided Liffey.

If she was discovered and had to explain to the voices *why* she was hiding under their room service cart, she would simply say she got lost, do her cover girl smile, and leave the room with as much dignity as she could muster.

She was tempted to peer out from under the cart to see if the voices belonged to the twins. Instead she eased quietly out from under it, trying not to obviously ruffle the tablecloth covering, and surveyed her surroundings.

She discovered she was in a little entrance hallway and not inside the room itself where the girls were still talking about the dances they were going to do the next morning. The chattering girls did not seem to be interested in the cart. "They probably think it's full of healthy snacks like carrots and celery that their mothers are going to force-feed them later," thought Liffey, who had not noticed any interesting smells while she had been hiding on the bottom shelf of the cart.

Liffey was tempted once again to look around the cart into the room to see if the girls she had heard talking were the twins, but thought better of it.

She crawled stealthily towards the door and listened for nearby voices outside in the hall. The way things were going today, she knew it would be just her luck to bump into someone returning *to* the room just as she was sneaking *out* of it!

Pressing her ear against the heavy metal door and hearing nothing, Liffey carefully opened the door and slipped out undetected into the main hallway. She felt like she had been given a second chance.

Liffey calculated that at least fifteen minutes must have gone by since she had last seen the skunk man waiting for the elevator on the 6th floor landing. She wondered if he actually *had* gotten back on the elevator, or if he had been lurking in the stairwell instead. Either way, he would have given up waiting for her by now. The coast should be clear.

Assuming that the skunk man had *not* seen her running to the food cart and hiding under it, and there was no reason to believe that he had, he would have to think that she actually *did* have some place to go when she had gotten on the elevator with him and was not just sneaking around spying on him.

Liffey decided that it was now safe to go back to the elevators and return to the lobby. She squeezed herself into the first one that stopped. It was packed with people, but Liffey was too deep in thought to notice the "You have *got* to be kidding!" looks she received from some of the passengers as she flattened herself against the glass wall, trying to make herself fit into the crowded elevator.

When she reached the lobby, Liffey resumed her power-walking to get ready for the feis. She did not want to let the skunk man ruin her focus and pre-feis warm-ups.

"Besides, maybe he was not after me at all and was just getting back on the elevator because he had forgotten something in the lobby." This thought comforted Liffey a great deal.

Maybe, as her father often pointed out, she was letting her imagination run away with her. But then, why did she keep getting the pins and needles feeling?

Liffey had learned to rely upon them. She knew they were telling her to *watch her step* and stay away from the skunk man!

# CHAPTER SIX
## Ignored

Liffey walked briskly along the Mark Twain hallway past the large windows of the hotel conference rooms. Inside the long, narrow rooms there were ceili teams practicing for tomorrow's figure dance competitions.

She slowed her pace when she saw her own school's name posted at the Jazz Room entrance and then stopped to watch the rehearsal.

There were three teams practicing inside. One of them was a U-13 team with girls from her own class running through their "Trip to the Cottage" figure dance, for what was probably the "millionth time," Liffey thought sympathetically.

She did not want to remain at the windows and stare at the obviously frustrated dancers going over and over their figure dances. "They look like they already have *enough* problems," Liffey observed, as she watched several false starts, a few un-pointed toes and two falls.

She hoped the fallen dancers were not hurt. One of them was crying and holding her ankle. "What do they *expect* when they name dances things like '*Slip*' Jig and '*Trip*' to the Cottage?" Liffey thought disgustedly. "They *totally* jinx dancers with names like that."

Continuing her power-walking, Liffey tried to figure out why she was always so miffed when she thought about all the dancers her own age who were already so far ahead of her.

Liffey did not really care very much about not being on a ceili team because she was used to being alone everywhere. But the fact that so many girls her age were so far ahead of her in their *solo steps* competitions made Liffey nuts sometimes! She did not begrudge them their own success. She just wanted to be successful too!

What made Liffey even more miserable than being behind in her solo steps was the fact that no one *ever* talked to her. There didn't seem to be anyone in Irish dance who wanted to become friends with her. Liffey was lonely. She was tired of talking to herself everywhere she went.

It seemed logical to Liffey that the reason she behaved so peculiarly and growled at dancers and breathed strangely at their mothers on the elevators, was because she was so *frustrated*! She wanted to be *advancing* in her steps but never got any help from the teachers or drillers at her school. Her Novice class was *huge* and she did her steps in the very back of it. She felt totally ignored and friendless.

Liffey could have easily afforded to pay one of the more advanced, older dancers for private lessons, but she lived too far away for that to happen easily. As it was, she had to be driven to class on Tuesday nights by her father's law office chauffeur because Robert Rivers never got back from Chicago before 8:00 p.m. each day. And the chauffeur had to *stay* there and wait for Liffey while she danced. Everybody noticed him outside waiting for her in the big white Mercedes.

It was very embarrassing, but Liffey and her father could not think of any other way to get her to the weekly class. There were two local taxi cab companies in the small Wisconsin town where she lived. However, the drivers were strange looking and gave the impression that they might never have ever left the city limits where they operated their cabs. So it was the chauffeur, or no Irish dance lessons.

Liffey was used to no one in her dance class talking to her, but none of the mothers of the dancers in her class had ever bothered to speak to her either.

Except one.

Once.

About a year ago, a mother had said: "Hello, *Shannon*. How are you today?"

Liffey was sure that if *her* mother were still alive, she would smile and greet every dancer that she saw going to or from class. *Her* mother would have noticed if a dancer seemed to be all alone and unhappy and *her* mother would have not called someone by the wrong name.

Liffey had started Irish dancing when she was eleven-years-old. "In Irish dance," Liffey complained to her father, "that is like starting when you're sixty-five."

Liffey could not help feeling somewhat resentful towards her father when she knew that some of the girls her own age had started dancing not long after they had learned to walk. No *wonder* they were so far ahead of her. Liffey could never get up enough nerve to actually confront her father, but she suspected that before her mother died, her mother would have made her father *promise* to give Liffey Irish dance lessons before she had even started kindergarten. Not junior high!

Liffey was a Novice. It had taken her two dance years to get to the Novice level. Even though she had routinely placed 1st and 2nd in all of her Advanced Beginner steps, nobody taught her the more complex Novice steps for another entire year. She *still* had not been taught a Novice Hornpipe, even though she got a 1st place in it the very first time she had done it at the Chicago Feis at the Advanced Beginner level.

By now Liffey was totally bored dancing in the Advanced Beginner Hornpipe competitions. She had begun to register (without permission) for the U-13 *Novice* Hornpipes and to do her Advanced Beginner Hornpipe steps with the U-13 Novice Hornpipe dancers. Liffey usually got a 5th place (if she placed at all) in it because her steps were *way* too easy for a Novice competition.

The Novice Hornpipers would furiously pound the stage and leap off the floor like grasshoppers all around her while Liffey just tried to blend in.

Liffey tried to conceal from the Novice Hornpipe judges how easy her steps were. She made as much noise as she could with *her* feet, like the other dancers, and held her breath until she turned blue. This would usually alarm the stage judge and cause more concern about her health than her dancing.

However, Liffey realized she had to eventually learn a Novice Hornpipe because she could not just keep holding her breath indefinitely. Next year, if she had won her solo dress, and *still* had not been taught a Novice Hornpipe, she would try wearing an "Arch" crown instead of holding her breath.

The main issue in Liffey's life was that she wanted a solo dress *now*! And it seemed hopeless because her school's Irish dance teachers didn't even know she was alive. Liffey knew she needed extra attention to work on the "little things" with her steps if she was ever going to win a first place in Novice. Like her turn out and making sure her steps were sharp and precise. And her knees. There was something about them too but she wasn't sure exactly what.

Liffey *was* sure, that if her own mother were still alive, she would have started Liffey's Irish dance lessons when Liffey was five or six and by now she would be right up there with the solo dress dancers. Liffey tried hard not to indulge in too much self-pity, but it was difficult not to be disheartened watching all the solo dresses walking around at competitions and St. Patrick's Day shows.

Liffey had been very disappointed at first to be so ignored in her Irish dancing classes, but then, she was used to being invisible.

At her Wisconsin middle school, she told her weary father one day after dinner when he questioned her as to why she never received any phone calls and never made any either: "It's because I don't fit in to any of the groups at school. I'm not popular. I'm not a geek. I'm not a druggie. I'm not a jock. I'm not *anything*. I'm just *there*. If I never went back to classes again, probably no one would even notice I was gone." Liffey saw the look of anguish on her over-worked father's face and so she quickly added, "But I love school. It rocks."

He looked very relieved and went back to writing his law brief at the kitchen table.

Liffey swallowed the tears that were beginning to make her nose bubble and quickly asked to be excused. She had decided long ago never to let her father know how miserable she really was.

# CHAPTER SEVEN
## Lilacs

Liffey's mother had died ten years ago when Liffey was only three-years-old. There were many photographs of baby Liffey and toddler Liffey with her young mother. The few video tapes she had of her mother were made shortly after Liffey was born. By the time she was one-year-old, her mother was sick and no more tapes were made.

Liffey's favorite family photo was the one taken right before her mother died. Her mother was snuggling close to her, holding little Liffey on her lap in a yard full of purple and white lilac bushes in full bloom. Her father was standing behind them with a sad little smile on his face. Liffey was smiling broadly, completely unaware that this would be the last time her mother posed for a photo with her.

Trying to remember her mother always brought a feeling of softness in someone's arms and the scent of lilacs, like the ones that grew along the side of her house every spring.

On May mornings, Liffey would always get up early before school and go outside to inhale their lovely fragrance. While the flowers still had overnight dew on them, she would press her nose into the pale purple blossoms and the water droplets would run down her cheeks like little tears.

This lilac ritual always made Liffey smile. She loved the spring, because unlike the other seasons, it brought a little bit of her mother back to her each year.

Liffey did not remember her mother's death or even how her father was after it. She only knew that there was a kind of emptiness in her life that seemed to have always been there.

Her mother's name was Maeve.

Liffey's father said her mother was named after Queen Maeve, a famous Irish warrior queen who was buried in her armor, *standing up*, on top of a mountain in Ireland. The mountain, called Knocknarea, was supposed to be hollow and have fairies living inside. Liffey was determined to go there someday and find them.

There was an oil painting of her mother above the fireplace in the living room. It showed a beautiful woman with light brown hair and big blue eyes sitting on a couch with her hands folded on her lap. But it was stiff and formal. It did not bring the softness of her mother to Liffey when she looked at it like the lilacs did each spring.

Liffey thought that the artist who painted that portrait of her mother should have put her mother in Queen Maeve's armor and had her standing on top of the fairy mountain bathed in moonlight. Her mother *should* have been holding up a battle shield, instead of sitting there on a couch with her hands politely folded.

# CHAPTER EIGHT
## A Feis Father

L iffey continued her power-walking, hoping to spot someone she recognized from her school in the crowded lobby. She thought again about the skunk man. Liffey was sure he was not a feis judge. Some of the adjudicators were pretty scary looking but not *that* scary!

She could not stop thinking about the *look* on the skunk man's face before the elevator doors closed and the fact that she *saw him* waiting to get back *on* the down elevator. She was fairly certain that *he* was snooping around now looking for *her*, just as she had done with him. "If only Daddy were here," sighed Liffey, "he would be able to size up the skunk man."

\*\*\*

Liffey's father, Robert Rivers, was a prominent criminal defense attorney. His office in Chicago's Loop, took up two full floors of space. There were marble walls and shiny golden handrails on the stairs and real hand towels in the restrooms with a fancy "R.R." stitched on them.

For several weeks after Liffey's mother had died, before her father made arrangements for child care, Liffey used to play in his huge law office conference room.

Sometimes her father would let her hide under his desk. Once, when Liffey had hidden under her father's desk without his permission, she listened to a long conversation her father had with an old man who had been accused of stealing a lot of money.

The man told her father that he did not steal anything and that her father had to help him stay out of jail. After the old man left the office, Liffey jumped out from underneath her father's desk and told a very startled Robert Rivers that the man he had been talking with was *lying* to him!

Her father was well aware that young Liffey could not have understood much, if anything, of the conversation she had been listening to underneath his desk. He asked her *how* she could possibly know the man had not been telling the truth.

Attorney Rivers was indignantly informed by his daughter that she *knew* this because she was all Irish on her mother's side, and that she, like her mother, had four eyes: two for "seeing" and two for "feeling."

\*\*\*

Heading back to the lobby network of connecting hallways, Liffey heard unanswered cell phones ringing all over the room. They reminded her that she needed to call her father tonight from the phone in her room.

Her father told her he did not want her to use her own cell phone at the hotel because she might lose it. But Liffey suspected it was for some other reason. She had heard him talking on the phone when he was making her hotel reservation, and he had used phrases like "for security reasons," and something about "signals," and the "wrong people" listening in. Liffey had *no* idea *what* he was talking about, but she had promised him not to use her cell phone at the feis and to keep it in her backpack for use at the airport only.

After Liffey had walked around the hotel lobby and its network of hallways fifty times, she felt the first wave of sleepiness come over her. Reluctantly, she knew it was time to go back to her room and turn in for the night.

Taking care to obey her father's orders to be accompanied to her room by hotel personnel, Liffey stopped at the front desk and asked for the concierge. The desk clerk made a quick phone call and this time, a few minutes later, a young woman in a band uniform came up behind Liffey and tapped her lightly on the shoulder. Her name tag said "Louise," like in *"Geez Louise!"*

Liffey was not in the mood to growl or hiss at Louise or anyone else at the moment, so she simply smiled and walked quietly to the elevators with the new concierge.

Liffey tried to shake the tight feeling in her chest caused by the skunk man's cold, hard stare earlier that night. She was tempted to tell Louise about her suspicion that something was *wrong* with the skunk man and his doll, but decided it would not be a good idea. Louise might tell her father and then Liffey might be ordered to stay put in her room until her father could come and take her home again.

"That would be bad," decided Liffey. "I *really* need to dance tomorrow."

Back in her room, the message light on the telephone next to her bed was flashing. "It's got to be Daddy," thought Liffey as she picked up the phone and pressed 1 for message waiting. She was right. It was Robert Rivers. But the voice mail her father had left utterly confused her: "Liffey, you left the hotel lobby this evening without getting an escort at the front desk and got on an elevator alone! Do *not* do that again young lady or this will be the *last* feis that you ever attend without me or your Aunt Jean! Love you anyway! Dad."

Liffey was stunned. She *had* followed the skunk man into the elevator and *had* ended up hiding under that cart inside of that room before she had managed to get back down to the lobby again. But how on *earth* did her father *know* she had gotten on that elevator without an escort? How could he *possibly* know? She *did* get an escort before coming back to her room. Her father must have known that too because he didn't mention it. He also did not mention the cart episode. Liffey *really* hoped he did not know about the cart!

When Liffey had followed the skunk man on to the elevator earlier to spy on him, she had not bothered to go to the hotel desk and ask for the concierge. If she had done that, she would have missed the elevator and never discovered the sparkling solo dress crown on the Irish dancer doll.

The plain truth was that Liffey had *forgotten* all about her father's rule because she was so *sure* she *had* to follow the skunk man! She had followed him by *instinct*, like a dog following a piece of steak. She had not stopped to think about the possible consequences of going up in the elevator without an escort then, because she did not plan on going back to her room.

Liffey dialed home slowly, anticipating a stern lecture from her father. Instead, he had left voice mail telling her he loved her and wishing her good luck in the morning. He had apparently gone to bed early, exhausted from his work day which usually began at 4:30 a.m. "Whew!" Liffey breathed a sigh of relief, "saved."

Liffey hoped that by tomorrow when she called home to report on the competition results, her father would have forgotten all about being upset with her.

# CHAPTER NINE
## Aunt Cheerleader

L iffey could not even *imagine* how *hideous* it would be to have to go to a feis with either her father or her Aunt Jean ever again!

\*\*\*

Her father had gone to the Chicago Feis with her the first year she started competing in Irish dance. He had acted like he was running for president or something, walking around smiling at everyone and shaking hands with them as he introduced himself. He kept pointing out Liffey to his victims as she stood in long lines waiting for her turn to dance. He talked to parents and other feis spectators like they were on a witness stand during a jury trial. He did not really talk *to* them. As Liffey recalled, he talked *at* them and interrogated them with questions like: "So, does your dancer regularly comply with the rules of the Irish Dance Teachers Association of North America?" Liffey still could not *believe* she heard him ask a feis mother that weird question while he was waiting for Liffey to dance.

Later, she asked him what kind of a conversation was *that*, asking some feis mom he had never even *seen* before if she "complied" with something that Liffey had never even heard of. His eyes twinkled as he explained that he was just trying to strike up a conversation and be friendly.

*** 

And Aunt Jean? Aunt Jean was not even *human*. Liffey strongly suspected she was from another planet.

Aunt Jean was her father's sister. She was a former beauty queen and cheerleader who did not seem to understand that Irish dance was not a pom pom squad.

She would yell things like: "Kick em HIGH, Kick em LOW, Liffey, Liffey, GO! GO! GO!" Liffey still cringed when she remembered the one and only feis that her Aunt Jean had come to with her. Her aunt had worn spiked heels that sunk into the grass as she walked around the feis grounds with Liffey, and way, way too much make-up. And that hideous hat! Aunt Jean had worn that awful, gross, ugly, floppy black hat. Then she had yelled that insane cheer while Liffey was *dancing*, totally unaware that feis rules did not allow cheering for dancers!

The adjudicator at the Slip Jig stage had looked too shocked to disqualify Liffey. Probably, only because the judge did not know *who* "Liffey" was, since all the dancers were wearing their feis numbers and not their names. Fortunately, there were so many dancers at the "Aunt Jean" feis that the stage judges were pretty overwhelmed, judging dancers in threes instead of twos. The second that Slip Jig ended, Liffey did her bows with the other two dancers who looked confusedly at each other and at Liffey, wondering which one of the three of them was *the* "Liffey."

Liffey did not hang around for the aftermath. She jumped off the stage and escaped into the crowd of waiting-to-dance dancers and their families.

"That must be how the Slip Jig got its name," Liffey mumbled to herself, as she tried to slip away before a stage monitor could find her and ask her if her name was *Liffey*.

Liffey made her father promise not to ever, *ever* let Aunt Jean accompany her to another feis. It was not that she did not love or respect her aunt. She did. She just never wanted her aunt anywhere even *near* a feis ever again. Liffey had enough to think about at a feis without worrying about what her aunt was going to do or say next.

*** 

Liffey kept the drapes open in her dark hotel room so she could look out at the Arch reflecting the night lights of St. Louis while she waited for sleep to come.

She thought again about the black-haired twins and their trophies and the skunk man, and then, just as she passed into the moment right before sleep and dreams, she remembered the smile on her mother's face and felt little popping kisses on her eyelids.

Next, Liffey was standing on a box holding a *huge* trophy! She was smiling and waving to the cheering crowd, while the twins, who had placed 2nd and 3rd at the Nationals, were looking up at her standing *between* them on the *first place* platform, trying to hide the astonishment on their faces.

# CHAPTER TEN
## Suiting Up

*C*rash!

Liffey woke up when she fell out of bed at 6:30 a.m. before her alarm went off. This often happened to her in hotels, so she would always be sure to sleep on the side of the bed which was opposite the telephone bed stand to avoid hitting her head on the way down to the floor.

Liffey stretched herself up from the floor like a cat, trying to loosen up her tight muscles before she was completely awake.

There was still an hour until the registration desk opened downstairs. It was time for the "feis breakfast."

Liffey opened the small room refrigerator and saw that her father must have ordered half the food in St. Louis! There was an *enormous* quantity of food packed into it. "How much food does he think I can put away in twenty-four hours?" Liffey laughed, looking at a full bag of apples, two big chunks of cheese, grape juice packets, turkey lunch meat, a bag of bagels and one huge tomato.

Mr. Rivers knew that his daughter liked to eat a bagel with melted cheese and a slice of tomato and turkey before she danced, so he had ordered the food to be delivered before she had even arrived in St. Louis.

What Mr. Rivers did *not* know, was that Liffey *had* to eat a bagel with melted cheese and a slice of tomato and turkey for her pre-feis breakfast, or she might jinx her dancing!

This morning, as she ate her good luck, pre-feis breakfast, she looked dreamily past the Arch at the majestic Mississippi River. Liffey could see herself and her father on the raft they had built themselves with tree branches from their own backyard. They were floating down the river with Tom Sawyer and Huck Finn on a lazy summer afternoon, dangling their feet in the water and telling jokes. They were all great friends.

Liffey was jolted back to reality with her alarm clock's 7:00 a.m. wake up call. It was time to begin another feis day! She rummaged through her backpack for her purple plastic disc inhaler. The chemicals inside it kept Liffey's asthma under control. Inhaling the disc mist deeply into her lungs, she held her breath and felt the first twinge of nervous excitement before she danced.

She was *ready* for this feis! She tried not to think about the fact that if she got a first place in any of her competition steps today, she would qualify for her first solo dress. She would just do her best.

Liffey carefully pulled on her poodle socks and used the sock glue she *finally* remembered to bring with her this time, to glue the white, bumpy socks to her legs. Her father thought that sock glue was crazy. Really off the wall crazy. He could not *believe* that Irish dancers *glued* their socks to their legs.

Next she slipped her feet into her soft shoe ghillies and began to lace them up. Her father never did figure out how it was done. Liffey had watched the older girls lacing up their shoes when she started Irish dance, and by the time she was ready to wear her first pair, she knew how tightly they must be fitted, and how to lace them up and then pull on the long string ties to secure them.

Her own ghillie laces had never *once* come undone during a competition and she was very proud of that. Especially proud, when she occasionally observed a distraught feis mom watching a daughter dance with untied ghillie strings flying all over the stage.

Liffey flexed her foot muscles and walked around the room like a duck to help her turnout. She *needed* to get her solo dress! Then she could wear *it* instead of her cumbersome school dress.

\*\*\*

Liffey did not think that her school dress was particularly attractive. In fact sometimes, depending on her mood, she thought it was really ugly. It was too dark. And it was made out of heavy, uncomfortable wool that was scratchy. She thought she looked like a nun in it, except the dress had pink, white and gold Celtic designs on it, all squiggled together like knots in a rope. There was too much color for a nun's habit. Surprisingly, Aunt Jean had liked the rope design on Liffey's dress.

At the Illinois Feis, after her aunt had almost gotten Liffey disqualified, they walked around together comparing dance school costume designs. Liffey had felt very mature and kind of like a "tour guide" of Irish dance dresses, explaining to her aunt that most Irish dance school costumes had embroidered designs on them which were inspired by decorations from an Irish copy of the Bible's New Testament. It was called: *The Book of Kells*.

Liffey informed her aunt that these valuable manuscripts were kept under glass, in a long case at Trinity College in Dublin, like Snow White sleeping after she ate the poisoned apple. There were a zillion Celtic designs in *The Book of Kells*. She taught her Aunt Jean a rhyme to remember the names of the four evangelist authors, whose work the monks had so lovingly copied in *The Book of Kells*: "Matthew, Mark, Luke and John, went to bed with their pajamas on!" Since it kind of sounded like a cheer, Liffey was sure her aunt would be able to remember it!

Aunt Jean, who still remained clueless as to her very bizarre feis behavior, had surprised Liffey with a beautiful copy of *The Book of Kells* for Christmas last year. There were colorful birds, and mythological-looking beasts with bulging eyes, and probably miles of Celtic knots, all carefully drawn by Irish monks who spent their entire *lives* decorating their manuscripts.

Just like Liffey was spending her entire life designing her solo dress.

*The Book of Kells* was beautiful. It was nothing like the dark, gloomy Bible that sat in her father's library at home on what Liffey called the "tomb table."

The tomb table Bible had Liffey's mother's name written in it, followed by her date of birth and then, her date of death. Inside the Bible there were also names and dates about people Liffey knew nothing about. She had never even heard of most of them. When she was five, her father had caught Liffey trying to erase her mother's name in the family Bible. She told him that she was going to *erase* her mother's name so that her mother would not be dead anymore.

Her father had gently removed the eraser from her chubby little fingers and told her that it was not that simple. Liffey wondered if the monks who did all the beautiful artwork in *The Book of Kells* had their own names entered in the chapters they had so tediously copied and decorated.

*** 

Finally, there was the school dress cape which was fastened by tying it to the dress just below the waist. It was kind of like anchoring a sail on a boat. Liffey's father thought it was ridiculous to anchor a cape and what purpose was there to even *having* a cape on a dress if it had to be fastened down anyway? Liffey told him that she was an Irish dancer, and that if she did *not* secure her cape she would look like a *flying squirrel* when she did her Slip Jig or Reel. They both cracked up when Liffey demonstrated the flying squirrel look and did her Slip Jig on their large backyard deck with the untied cape sailing behind her like an airborne kite.

Clock check: According to the clock radio, it was already 7:25 a.m. Time to go!! Liffey put on a little mascara and lip gloss and slipped her room key into her dance bag.

***

**BAG CHECK:**

Sock glue

Extra poodle socks in case feet bleed from unbroken in new hard shoes.

Duct tape in case feet get blisters.

Salve for possible blisters.

Bottled water (two)

Emergency inhaler in case breathing acts up.

Black elastic bands for hard shoes to hold them in place.

Teach Yourself Spanish book to study in results room.

Chewing gum for nerve control between stages.

Hershey Bar for quick carbo hit if needed.

Pen, to check off stages in feis registration book.

Moist towels for unexpected stickiness from Hershey Bar.

***

Everything seemed to be in the bag that she could possibly need. "That means I *must* have forgotten something," worried Liffey. She was a firm believer in Murphy's Law: "What *can* go wrong, *will* go wrong!" Every time!

As she slipped her arms into the "You *must* wear it or else!" cover-up smock, she kept having the feeling that she was forgetting something really important.

Liffey felt ridiculous wearing the smock but her dance school rules demanded that all dancers wear dress smock cover-ups when they were not dancing. Liffey thought the little girl dancers looked adorable all smocked-up but she herself felt totally *stupid* wearing hers. Like a big baby with a bib.

Still, she always wore the smock in spite of feeling stupid because she did not know what actually might *happen* to her if she was seen without it. Probably nothing, but she did not want to find out!

Finalizing her departure to the feis world below, she remembered to remove her cell phone from her dance bag. Liffey never brought her cell phone with her to the dance stage areas because she had lost two of them already and her father told her if she lost *one more* she would not get another one until she was twenty-one. Anyway, this time her father had ordered her not to use her phone in the hotel at all.

As she walked towards the room phone to call the front desk and request a concierge escort, she stopped to do one final inspection in the full-length mirror on the bathroom door:

Socks were even.

Make up looked good.

Her hair?

Ouch!

*Really* bad! A really, really bad hair day!

"Wait a minute! Where's my wig? I *forgot* my wig?" screeched Liffey.

Liffey fervently hoped that forgetting to put on her wig was not an omen of the day to come! Would she forget her steps too?

She quickly removed the smashed up wig from its Tupperware container. Breaking her own record, she pony tailed her hair and had the wig securely positioned and fastened with *extra* bobby pins in thirty-five seconds. She centered her dance school headpiece. *Now* she was ready to begin her second Celtic Arch Feis!

Satisfied with her appearance, Liffey called the front desk and asked for her escort to the lobby. She sat on the bed waiting for the concierge to arrive and practiced pointing her toes until they ached. After hundreds of ankle flexes, there was a knock at the door.

She peeked through the peep hole and was pleased to see that it was Louise again. Liffey liked Louise because she was natural and easy to be with. Not stiff and formal like Bert. Opening the door, she gave Louise a genuine smile and did a leap over out into the hall.

Liffey was determined to do her best and earn her first place medal today!

Louise followed from behind, deliberately keeping a distance between them. As Louise watched Liffey approach the elevator and push the down arrow, she lowered her chin and spoke into a small microphone which was concealed inside the ornate concierge collar on her uniform. Looking at her watch, Louise carefully dictated the date, time and place.

They entered the elevator together and Liffey immediately exchanged the genuine smile with which she had greeted Louise, for her standard elevator cover girl smile. Liffey hissed a little on the way to the lobby at two feis mothers who were pretending not to look at her and Louise. Louise did not seem to notice Liffey's little eccentricities.

When they reached the lobby level, Louise wished Liffey good luck and told her to make sure she called for her at the concierge desk when she went *anywhere* other than the lobby or dance stage areas. Liffey promised that she would, took a deep breath and headed towards the loud crowd in the registration area.

What a din! The lobby was already full of nervous, wigged dancers and their even more nervous, chattering mothers. There was the smell of fresh coffee and hairspray in the air conditioned lobby air.

Some of the advanced dancers were pounding the tiled floors in their hard shoes, practicing their treble jigs and hornpipes. Other dancers were stretching on the floor, oblivious to almost entirely blocking the hallways. Still others were leaping around the lobby like it was dance class. It all looked routine and familiar to Liffey. She could hear fiddlers tuning their violins in the distance and a tin whistle player warming up. It was feis day and she and the other dancers were all running on nervous excitement!

Doing a quick lobby check, Liffey spotted a snobby girl from her dance school who pretended not to see her as she passed right by Liffey on her way to the registration desk. They were in the same dance class together and had been for two whole years. But the girl had never *once* spoken to Liffey, either in class, or out of class and *especially* not at a feis!

\*\*\*

At first, Liffey tried hard to be nice to the snobby girl saying things like: "Where did you get that cute shirt?" and "I love your hair!" The snob had replied with a pathetic, anemic smile and then had deliberately turned away from Liffey to talk to the other dancers in the class. The ones who were not *invisible* like Liffey.

Liffey no longer even tried to talk to the snobby girl. Now Liffey growled at her in dance class instead. This caused the unfriendly girl to look down at the floor and twist her hair nervously through her fingers.

Liffey was seriously considering wearing her dog Max's muzzle to dance class some Tuesday night. That would have to terrify her fellow novices. It might even cause her teachers to watch her dance for a change.

# CHAPTER ELEVEN
## To Jig or Not To Jig

Liffey waited in line at the letter "R" section of the registration table. When she was handed her registration packet and feis competitor number, she was delighted to see that the piece of cardboard with her number on it said 678. This was a *really* good sign!

Liffey's theory about feis numbers, was that if she got a competition number that was numerically in order counting both ways, like a 123, or backwards, 321, it was very good luck. Happily, she tied the lucky, already hole-punched 678 competition number around her waist with the string she found in her registration packet.

According to the feis manual, the day would start with the Jig step as usual. Liffey did it well, but as in her other Novice steps, she had not yet won a first place in it.

Liffey read for the trillionth time, the rules outlining how dancers reach the different levels of Irish dance. Robert Rivers had studied these rules and regulations and had finally given up trying to figure it all out. He said people should be sent to college to get a degree in "Feis Science" before they were asked to interpret the rules and regulations of the feis world. "If a lawyer cannot make any sense out of it, then who can?" he had asked his daughter.

All Liffey knew, was that she *had* to get a first place in one of her Novice steps to get a solo dress. She would worry about the other levels later.

Liffey did not even dare to imagine what it must be like getting *two first places* at the Prelim level and qualifying for the Championship level. Her first task was to get her solo dress! And that meant she needed to read her feis program book right now to find out where all the stages were located.

She followed the feis manual's map along the hallway to the stage where the Novice U- 13 dancers would eventually be checking in. When she found it, Liffey could see that the stage judge had not yet arrived and nothing seemed to be happening. *That* was no surprise. Sometimes Liffey waited a very long time at a stage for an adjudicator to arrive. Once, a whole minivan of adjudicators were hours late because their driver got lost between their hotel and the feis grounds.

Liffey thought that one of the worst things that could happen to a dancer at a feis was when it was *finally* your turn to dance and then the whole feis would just *stop* for lunch! Just stop. Then there was nothing to do but wait around the stage being nervous until the judge finished eating or napping. Liffey supposed that the judges deserved to eat and possibly nap, but not when it was *her* turn to dance!

Liffey counted competitions and figured out that the U- 13 Novice Jig was the third competition from the beginning. Knowing from previous feis experience that it could easily be a good two hours or more before her age group started to dance, Liffey decided to explore the feis shopping area.

Since the judge was not even there yet, and the other two competitions were split into A and B groups of twenty-five dancers each, that meant there were one hundred dancers who would be dancing before it was her turn!

"How can a judge remain *awake* watching all those dancers all day long?" Liffey's father had asked, after the one and only feis he had been to with her. Her father did not think it was possible.

Liffey did not know how the judges stayed awake either. A few times, she was sure a judge had nodded off. Once, she actually heard an adjudicator snoring! That was one reason she was not overly discouraged about not having won a 1st place in a Novice step yet. She didn't blame the judges for falling asleep!

\*\*\*

During her first year of competing, after not placing even *once* at the Milwaukee Feis, Liffey had dejectedly gone into a snack bar for a sympathy lunch. A nice young mother sitting close to her at another table with her tiny beginner dancer could see how upset Liffey was. When the mother asked her if it was a bad day, Liffey told her that this feis had been a total, complete *bust*.

The young feis mother's reply still inspired Liffey on bad days. She said: "You know, sometimes when I used to dance, I placed when I *really* didn't *deserve* to place. And then sometimes, when I really, really, really did well and *totally deserved* to be first, I didn't even *place*! But what I found, is that it all seems to even itself out in the end. So you hang in there and don't let the days you did not get what you deserved get you down.

Your day will come if you work hard and stay with it." Liffey knew that her own mother would have been just like that kind lady.

\*\*\*

Liffey started out from the Jig stage and headed towards the feis shopping area. She looked through the gathering crowd and saw no familiar faces. No twins. No Tuesday night class members. And most importantly, no skunk man! Liffey had kept an eye out for the skunk man ever since she had arrived in the lobby. So far, she had not seen him.

She continued on towards the large hotel ballroom where the vendors were setting up the usual supplies of Irish dancing hard shoes, ghillies, spankies, hair ties, poodle socks, jewelry, sock glue, silver buckles, zillions of T-shirts, sweat shirts, tin whistles, dance practice tapes and enough Irish novelty gifts for hundreds of St. Patrick's Day presents!

There was also a table with books and magazines but Liffey thought she had better wait to check out the books until *after* she had danced her Jig. Liffey had already missed the Jig step *twice* before at other competitions due to getting totally lost in a book and not getting to her Jig stage in time to dance it.

\*\*\*

Liffey's father had told her that she might be *deliberately* avoiding the Jig, even though she did not *know* she was deliberately avoiding it. He knew she was sick of doing the Jig step. He told Liffey that many of his criminal clients had convinced themselves that the crimes they had committed were accidental and not deliberate. He suggested that she think very seriously about *why* she kept missing the Jig, and that maybe it was not accidental.

"You should have been a shrink instead of a lawyer," Liffey proclaimed after one of his longer psychology lectures.

\*\*\*

As she walked into the shopping area spread out all over the large hotel ballroom like a mini-mall, Liffey was contemplating whether she really *was* unconsciously trying to miss the Jig again today, when she felt herself losing her balance on the slippery wooden floor beneath her. To her dismay, she was unable to break the fall, and felt her bottom slam down on the hard floor!

Liffey tried not to cry out. It hurt a lot and what hurt even more was her pride. How *stupid* she must look, losing her balance while walking in a straight line!

She glanced right, then left and was both relieved and angry when she realized that no one had seemed to notice.

"That figures," Liffey muttered to herself. "Why would anyone even care if I broke my leg? I would probably have to crawl out to the lobby and ask to use the desk phone to call 911 all by myself."

# CHAPTER TWELVE
## The Return of the Skunk Man

L iffey was feeling very sorry for herself and more than a little bit humiliated, when, to her utter amazement, directly to her left, underneath a table piled high with ghillies, she saw a shopping bag with a few curls peeking out. On top of the curls was a diamond solo dress crown. *"That's it! It's the same one!"* Liffey was ecstatic! *"That* is the shopping bag the skunk man had been carrying last night on the elevator!"

Liffey observed that the bag was under a shoe vendor's table and that he was *not* selling porcelain Irish dancing dolls. He was only selling shoes. Yet right under his table of dozens of hard shoes and possibly hundreds of ghillies, was that solo dress crown!

Liffey was certain that it was the same crown she had seen on the elevator, because the diamonds on it were sparkling even underneath the table in dim light.

"What on earth is the shopping bag doing under a shoe vendor's table?" Liffey felt giddy with excitement as she began to scoot along on her rear end towards it. The shopping bag was drawing her in like a whirlpool! After scooting only a few feet, however, a pair of large, black leather shoes stepped in between Liffey and the shoe table.

At first, Liffey did not notice them because her eyes were *totally* fixed on the shopping bag containing the incredible solo dress crown. She was too anxious to get to the shopping bag to notice the pins and needles which had started inching up and down her neck.

The next thing she knew, a sneering, raspy voice was talking to her!

"Can I *help* you get up little Irish dancer girl?" the creepy voice asked.

Liffey *knew* without even looking up that the harsh voice belonged to the skunk man! She instantly began to retreat from the danger she knew the shoes represented. Still on her sore rump, she was only dimly aware of how peculiar she must look to the early morning shoppers who were now watching her fleeing on her bottom, in full Irish dance dress, as she headed towards the ballroom exit.

She slid quickly along not daring to look up.

After she had managed to cover a few yards, Liffey pushed herself up from the floor, on to her feet and sprinted for the door. She did not look back.

Somehow Liffey made it to the Jig stage. Another nightmare! The U-13 Jig was *starting*! They must have decided to speed things up and had sent the younger dancers to another stage. A stage monitor looked at Liffey's number, quickly checked it off on the sign-in sheet, and gently pushed her on to the plywood stage with the ten other girls who had made it there on time for their U-13 Jig.

Liffey stood like a robot, while the other dancers stepped out in front of the judge and launched themselves into their Jig steps in pairs. Liffey realized that she was the odd number eleven in the line, so she would have to do her steps alone.

"No partner for Liffey! Oh well, what *else* is new?"

Liffey was very distracted and agitated as she stood there wondering where the skunk man was now and whether she would see him again after she finished her Jig. What would she do if she *did* see him again?

It was her turn. Automatically, Liffey stepped out of the line of dancers who had already done their Jigs, made sure her arms were like stiff boards at each side, and waited for the musician to begin playing his fiddle.

The music began. Liffey pointed her right foot and began to count.

JUMP, knee, hop back, two, three, four...she was jigging like she had never jigged before! Fear was making her steps precise, like scissors cutting paper.

The music ended. Like a robot, Liffey bowed to the judge, who nodded back at her. She turned and did a little bow to the fiddler. It was over.

*Then* she saw him. The skunk man! He was *right* there in the middle of the crowd. He must have been watching the U-13 Jig!

Unexpectedly, the skunk man turned into a blur and faded away. Liffey heard a thud and wondered if one of the dancers in back of her had slipped and fallen like she had done earlier this morning in the ballroom. "I hope she's not hurt," thought Liffey. Then there was total darkness. And the twins again. They were there smiling and waving.

# CHAPTER THIRTEEN
## Down but Not Out

When Liffey's eyes opened again, she saw two men wearing white jackets with large EMT letters. They were kneeling next to her on the Jig Stage floor. Louise, the concierge, was also kneeling next to her on the floor. *The floor!* Was she on the *floor?* "What in the world am I doing on the *floor?*" Liffey was stupefied.

She tried to explain to the EMT men and Louise that she did not know *why* they thought she wanted to be lying on the floor and that if she did not get to her next stage *right* away, she might *miss* her Slip Jig, and she could *not* miss it because it was her best shot at getting a first place today since she had totally messed up her Jig. And could they all *please,* just stand aside, so she could just go and *do* her Slip Jig, because it was her favorite step, even though she probably did the Jig step better, and she might actually be able to get her *Solo Dress* if they would just let her *go!*

"What is your name?" asked one of the EMT men.

Liffey looked at Louise for the correct answer. Louise said nothing. Certainly Louise would know who she was because her father had *hired* Louise to walk her to and from her room today. So why didn't Louise *tell* them who she was?

Louise remained mute. "O.K," grumbled Liffey. "O.K. I can do this. This is a *total* no-brainer. I will *tell* you who I am. I am the River Liffey," said Liffey matter-of-factly. "I am *not* the River Shannon." The men stared blankly at Liffey as she continued: "*You* know! I am that river in *Dublin*, not the *other* one."

"I see," said one of the white-coated men looking at Louise and the other EMT with a fixed frown on his face. "May we speak with your mother or father?" the man continued.

Liffey began to explain that her mother was above the fireplace at home and her father was in Chicago today when Louise finally spoke up. "Let's put her in the Arch Room while I find a wheelchair to get her to the nurse's station. I'll call her father and let him know what happened."

Liffey was surprised when she was lifted up by the two men and placed on a mobile stretcher. "Why am I on a *stretcher*?" "This is ridiculous!" Liffey objected.

Liffey knew she was going to have to recover her extensive vocabulary quickly if she were ever going to get away from these white coats and make it to her Slip Jig Stage in time to dance.

"Did I hit my head when I fell?" asked Liffey, back in control again.

"I don't think so," answered one of the white coats from behind her on the stretcher. "You were lucky I guess. You pretty much just slumped down gracefully into a little heap on the floor as it was described to us."

Liffey kept her eyes closed tightly as the stretcher procession began its trip to the Arch Room so she did not have to see all the people that she knew would be staring at her now more than ever. She was a little *heap* being carried off the stage like a football player on a stretcher. This was awful! And where was the skunk man *now*? Was he still watching her?

They must have finally arrived at the Arch Room because she noticed that the parade featuring herself on a mobile stretcher float all tucked up in a warming blanket had stopped. There were no more curious distant voices babbling in the background. It was quiet.

Liffey *had* to get rid of the white coats. She *had* to get to that shopping bag under the table before someone took it away!

She was fairly certain that when she had seen the skunk man in the crowd before she had slumped into blackness, he was standing with his arms folded in front of him. She was almost positive that he did not have the bag while he was watching her jig. How could she slip away from these well-meaning paramedics? She opened her eyes and looked around the room. There was only one door.

Just as Liffey was despairing as to how she was ever going to get out of the Arch Room, a beeper went off. "*Code Red!*" she heard an EMT exclaim. "We have to take it."

"Yes! Yes! They will have to answer that call and I can escape!" Liffey was *almost* out of there! She wondered what color *her* code had been when they had been beeped about the heap! Liffey giggled. That was actually almost funny! Beeped about the heap!

The men called out to her as they ran out of the room to answer the Code Red, assuring her that either they, or Louise, would be right back and for her to stay put.

"Take your time," Liffey answered.

# CHAPTER FOURTEEN
## Diamonds

Liffey stood up slowly and was happy to discover that she felt somewhat normal again. She was a little blank and somewhat dizzy but she was able to remember how old she was and that she was at the Celtic Arch Feis in St. Louis.

She knew why she had fainted when she was bowing to the musician. It was not because she was sick. It was because the shock of looking eyeball to eyeball with the skunk man had been too much for her!

*Why* had the skunk man tried to follow her *twice* now? She shivered remembering her near-escape on the elevator last night. If only she had not been so *obvious* on the elevator looking into the shopping bag at that diamond crown. What *was* it that the skunk man thought she knew or suspected?

All at once Liffey realized exactly *what* it was that she *did* know! Somehow she *knew* that the diamonds *looked* so *real* on the doll's solo dress crown because THEY WERE REAL!!! "That is why the skunk man is following me around! *That's* why I keep getting the crawly pins and needles up and down my back! He's a THIEF! And he thinks that I had figured it out last night on the elevator when I kept staring into his shopping bag. He's afraid I will *tell* someone about it," thought Liffey, realizing that the next step she must take *was* to tell someone about it!

Knowing what the skunk man was up to made Liffey

feel like she was walking on the edge of a cliff as she practiced walking, pacing herself to see if she was steady enough on her feet to escape from the EMT men. Her head hurt a little and she was shaking slightly, but it was probably from the excitement of realizing that she had figured out the skunk man's secret. Otherwise, she seemed to be able to walk normally again.

It was hard for Liffey not to be very, very afraid of the secret she had uncovered. She knew now that there was no way she could risk being caught by the skunk man. He might actually harm her if he thought she was going to tell the authorities about the diamond crown.

At the same time, Liffey also knew that she *had* to get that doll with the diamond crown if anyone was ever going to believe her story. She was grateful that her father had registered her in the hotel under the name "Mary Locke." She would be protected from the skunk man's finding out what hotel room she was staying in.

\*\*\*

Robert Rivers was an experienced criminal defense attorney. He knew how the criminal mind worked. Until Liffey had encountered the skunk man, she thought all of her father's precautions were silly and completely unnecessary. Now she was happy to be "Mary Locke!" If anyone were to go to the front desk and ask for Liffey Rivers' room, they would be told she was not registered at this hotel.

\*\*\*

Liffey thought again how vitally important it was to *get* that doll. If she did *not* get the doll, no one would ever believe her story about the skunk man chasing her around a hotel in St. Louis because she *knew* that he *knew* that she *knew* the diamonds on the doll's solo dress crown were *real* diamonds! She was afraid that it might already be too late.

Liffey was *sure* she had solved the mystery of the sparkling solo dress crown! It was an ingenious way to secretly move *real jewels* from point A to point B. Who would have imagined that a doll would be wearing *real* diamonds? But where in the world *were* these points? And *who* was moving the jewels between them?

Liffey needed to go one step further now to find out *where* that crown was headed. If she could figure *that* out, she might also learn where the jewels had come from in the first place. Then she could call her father and have the skunk man apprehended.

And why had the skunk man left the shopping bag under a *shoe vendor's* table? Was the vendor in on the diamond plot? Or was that just a drop place for someone else to pick up the doll?

***

Liffey thought she was walking steadily enough now to make her escape. She did *not* want the white coats coming back into the room and discovering her in another little heap. Feeling strong enough to sneak out, Liffey left the Arch Room undetected.

She kept to the side of the large crowd moving through the hallway and made sure that she walked erectly even though she felt weak and drained. "Irish dancers always walk like they have boards glued to their backs," she told herself. "I must walk with a purpose, like I am going to my next competition stage."

Liffey was also aware that she needed to mingle with the crowd or Louise might find her and make her get into a wheelchair and *then* what? Louise would probably call her father and she would end up being taken to an emergency room somewhere in St. Louis and the skunk man would get away and no one would ever go after him to find the jewels! Liffey feared that the skunk man might even be gone already. She needed to get back to that long shoe table to see if the shopping bag with the doll was still under it.

As Liffey crossed through the lobby and approached the entrance to the feis vendors' area, she tried to figure out where the solo dress crown was *going* after it left the hotel.

Liffey was well aware that in order to solve this mystery, she would first have to make sure that the crown did *not* leave this hotel until it had been examined by an expert who would be able to verify if the diamonds were real or fake.

She kept a sharp look out for the skunk man. If she saw him again and he came near her, she decided she would scream and yell "Help!" That would get the attention of every other dancer and their mothers and fathers in the entire building.

*** 

Liffey finally arrived at the shopping area. After quickly determining that the skunk man did not appear to be in the vendors' ballroom, she positioned herself at a table of T-shirts and pretended to look at the sizes.

The T-shirt table was directly in back of the shoe table where she had slipped and hit the floor earlier in the day. She squinted and tried to see if the shopping bag was still under it. She thought she *did* see something, so she pretended to keep looking at the T-shirts and kept her "spy-eyes," fixed on the dark shape under the shoe table. Liffey was almost sure it was *the* shopping bag!

Liffey was well aware that she had to be patient. She had

to resist the urge to run over to the table and grab the shopping bag and run. If she did do that, then *she* would be the thief and the skunk man might be able to get away with his diamond scheme!

She made up her mind that if someone came to pick up the shopping bag, she would run over to the shoe table and make a scene. She would say that the doll was *her* doll. Hotel security would be called to sort out the disturbance she had created. Then she could explain her theory about the crown, and request a police investigation to check out the crown before it left the hotel.

If the hotel security officers did not believe her, she would call her father and have him contact someone somewhere. He always knew what to do. She had to wait. And she had to be patient. She wished she had not obeyed her lawyer-father and left her cell phone in her room. If she had brought it with her, she could be calling him right now for legal advice.

Liffey kept her head down and hoped Louise would not come into the ballroom pushing a wheelchair with orders from her brilliant father to put her in it!

# CHAPTER FIFTEEN
## The Redheaded Woman

As Liffey continued to inspect T-shirt labels, she observed that the shoe table's one employee was so busy with feet fitting that he did not notice her peeking over at what Liffey was now *sure* was *the* shopping bag!

After about twenty minutes of hiding her face so Louise would not see her and keeping an eye out for the skunk man and looking at about a hundred small, medium and large labels, Liffey observed a pretty young woman with striking red hair walk up to the shoe table.

She watched the woman take out a wallet from the fanny pack she was wearing and hand an envelope to the vendor who seemed to know what she wanted. He reached under the table, picked up the shopping bag, and handed it over to the redheaded woman! Even at a distance, Liffey could see the crown on the little doll's head glittering under the ballroom's crystal chandeliers.

Liffey's patience had paid off! She swallowed hard trying to figure out what she should do next. Should she make a scene? The redhead did not look like a player in a diamond smuggling plan. On the other hand, Liffey knew she could *not* lose sight of that bag again!

She dropped the Xtra-large T-shirt she had been examining for the last ten minutes and waited until the redhead made a move. "She seems to know the shoe salesman," thought Liffey, as she watched them conversing easily together.

Approximately five minutes later, the woman finished talking to the shoe vendor and gracefully walked away, "just like an Irish dancer," Liffey noted, following the pretty young woman out into the hallway.

Relieved that there did not seem to be any sign of either the skunk man or Louise in the hall, Liffey continued to follow the lovely red curls into the hotel lobby. It seemed that the redhead was in a hurry as she briskly walked over to the far bank of elevators, which was not crowded for a change, and pushed the up arrow.

Liffey took after her. The diamond solo dress crown was barely visible in the shopping bag.

The redhead, who did not seem to notice Liffey, appeared to be around mid-twenties, Liffey decided, and "very pretty, not at all sinister looking like the skunk man."

This redhead obviously did not know that the diamonds on the doll's crown were real and probably part of some criminal plot. Liffey was certain that the redhead had been sent to get the shopping bag for someone else, like her boss or a friend. She looked very innocent and seemed to be totally unaware that she was carrying around a doll wearing a crown which could easily be worth millions of dollars!

Liffey debated with herself about telling the pretty redhead before they got on the elevator that the crown she was carrying might be very dangerous, but decided to wait until they both got off the elevator together.

The elevator reached the lobby. Liffey and the redheaded woman entered it together. The redhead pushed the number 12 button. Liffey pretended to study the row of floor buttons and then cheerfully said, "Oh, you already pushed it. I'm going to 12 too."

"This pretty redhead cannot know what she is doing,"

thought Liffey. "I will have to hope that she believes me when I tell her that she might be in danger carrying that shopping bag around for someone else."

The redhead smiled warmly at Liffey, who was *very* relieved to at last be with someone she thought she could trust. She made up her mind that she would first tell the redhead all about the skunk man and how he had been following her all over the hotel. Then she would go into her theory that the solo dress crown was made up of *real* diamonds as soon as they got off the elevator together on the 12th floor.

Liffey hoped that no one else would get on the elevator with them, and anxiously watched as the floor numbers passed by, getting closer and closer to the 12th floor where she could finally share her secret with someone! She would save this nice lady from being tricked into making a horrible mistake!

The elevator ride to the 12th floor seemed endless. When the 12th floor bell finally sounded, Liffey quickly stepped off the elevator and turned around excitedly to tell the redheaded lady all about her crown theory.

Instead, Liffey was flabbergasted when the doors of the elevator began to close and she heard the down bell sounding, announcing its departure. The redhead flashed a pleasant cover-girl-kind-of-smile at Liffey just as the elevator doors swished *shut*. Liffey was left standing there alone utterly confused. Did the redhead forget something downstairs? Liffey was entirely bewildered as she watched the overhead elevator lights signaling its downward path to the hotel lobby...11, 10, 9, 8....

Fully aware that she had to do *something* other than just standing there gaping at the elevator lights, Liffey quickly ran across the hall to the other elevator and pushed the down arrow. She noticed that this elevator was already on its way up, as the 6th floor and then the 7th floor lights blinked on and off.

If this elevator kept coming up without stopping, maybe she could get back down to the lobby in time after all to find the redhead before she got herself into trouble carrying the crown around in that shopping bag.

All at once, Liffey felt like she had just smashed into a wall of bricks! An overwhelming sense of dread came over her. She now understood what was actually going on here.

She had been *lured* into that elevator! The redheaded lady *knew* that Liffey would follow her to the elevators because she must be *working with the skunk man*!!!

# CHAPTER SIXTEEN
## Running

The prickly pins and needles began crawling up and down Liffey's back as she faced another horrifying possibility. *"What if the skunk man was on the elevator coming up?"* It was blinking past the 10th floor and there were only two floors left to do something. If it *was* the skunk man, and her warning signs said that it was, she *had* to get out of there immediately! But she was on the 12th floor and as far away from the lobby and safety as anyone could possibly be in this hotel!

Screaming would do no good here because she was not waiting for one of the glass cage elevators with their open levels all the way down to the main lobby. Those elevators only went as far as the 8th floor. Liffey had followed the redhead on to another set of elevators at the far end of the lobby that went up to the higher floors. They were the regular elevators that went up and down from the back of the hotel.

Liffey also knew that all of the rooms in this hotel were very sound proof and that someone would probably have to be coming out of their room into the hallway to even hear someone screaming. *And* there were little dancer screamers all over the hotel chasing each other around playing in the hallways. *And* dancers screaming if they got a 1st place at the feis today. No one would even notice if *she* started screaming! Not here. Not today.

Liffey felt completely boxed in as she frantically scanned the hallways feeding into the bank of 12th floor elevators and saw that no one was coming. She did not have time to run down the halls knocking on doors seeking sanctuary within a safe room.

There were no maids with their friendly carts piled high with linens to hide in. No room service cart to hide under this time. Liffey feared she might faint again if the elevator doors opened and the skunk man was standing there. She gathered every little bit of courage she could from within and remembered to put her thinking cap back on her head. She had to *run* right now! There was no time left to think!

As the up elevator passed right by the 11th floor, Liffey dashed towards the lighted red "Exit" sign a few feet from her on the left and opened the door. It was cool in the stairwell and she leaned against the cold concrete wall trying not to panic. She knew she *had* to move but she was paralyzed with fear. Her stomach was churning and she was afraid she might throw up. Instead, Liffey's automatic drive started and she felt her feet starting to walk carefully down the stairs. She clung to the cheap metal railing, taking each step noiselessly.

Doing her best to not dwell on the fact that she was in grave danger, she began to count the concrete steps going down to keep from screaming.

Or crying.

Or fainting.

"1, 2, 3, 4, 5, 6, 7, 8, 9, 10, 11...step on a crack and break your mother's back. I do not have a mother, so I do not have to obey the rhyme," Liffey whispered, scarcely breathing...12, 13, 14, 15, 16, 17, 18....

Was the door at the top of the steps quietly opening?

Liffey was sure she heard a little creaking noise like the

one her bedroom closet door made at home. Just a little creak. Then another. Then there was nothing. Had she imagined it? *Was* the skunk man in the stairwell, or did he leave when he did not see or hear anyone moving down it? Liffey moved to the wall. She was fairly certain that if she kept to the inside wall, instead of the metal railing, she would remain out of sight.

Liffey could not see the top of the stairwell. If she could not see *it*, then she could not be *seen*. Or so she hoped.

There was absolutely no sound whatsoever on the stairs except the hum of a vending machine vibrating through the thin wall she was leaning against, supporting her trembling body as she moved slowly down the narrow metal stairs.

She wondered whether it was Coke or Pepsi.

Maybe the skunk man was gone? He did not hear anything in the stairwell, so now he was on the 12th floor looking up and down the four intersecting hallways for her. Maybe she had eluded the skunk man after all! But the pins and needles still hurt from the warning feeling, so she knew she could not just assume that she had managed to get away from him.

It was obvious to Liffey that she would have to do something soon. She could not just keep slinking down the stairwell taking forever between steps. It was like *waiting* for the skunk man to sneak up on her! Hopefully, someone would come into the stairwell and then she could walk with them. But most people took the elevator when they were going down from the higher floors.

"Thank goodness I am still wearing my ghillies," Liffey thought. Wearing ghillies was almost as good as being barefooted because they made very little noise. And she had been trained by her Irish dance teachers to land quietly in them. That was one thing she had actually learned from last year's classes!

She *had* to keep moving to put more distance between herself and the skunk man. 19, 20..."I have to take two steps at a time," Liffey realized, "or it will take forever and I may never make it all the way down...21, 22, 23." She tried to remain level-headed as she moved away from the cool wall, back to the metal railing. She would use the railing like a gymnast doing bar work to project herself down the stairs, two at a time.

But before she could even attempt taking two stairs at a time, she heard him! He sounded like a herd of stampeding horses coming at her. The skunk man obviously did not care *how* much *noise he* was making! He had heard her sneaking down the stairs and was now determined to catch her!

Liffey gasped and took off like a jack rabbit, hopping down the stairs two at a time while she held on to the railing for balance. But the skunk man had long legs and they were closing in on her. Liffey stopped counting the stairs as she frantically leapt downward taking as many steps as she could without losing her grip and falling.

Unless she did something drastic, it was apparent that the skunk man would catch her soon. As she had feared, nobody entered the stairwell as she continued flying down the stairs. Liffey could not *believe* that in a hotel this big with so many guests, that not *one* of them had decided to take the stairs!

She wished she were taller and bigger so that she could jump over the railing and take the steps landing by landing.

Liffey knew it was now or never time *again* and that she had to immediately come up with some kind of way out of this or she would have to pay the consequences for having put herself in harm's way once more. She could almost see her father's horrified face when they told him that there had been an "accident" in the hotel stairwell.

Then it came to her! She would do what her father had

always said she should do if she ever found herself all alone and in desperate straits, "*SCREAM!*" Liffey could almost *hear* her father say it!

Liffey screamed so loudly that she almost lost her balance as she continued racing down the stairwell. She screamed and screamed like she did on the roller coasters at Great America and Kennywood on their biggest dips. The screams echoed and bounced all over the stairwell.

She stopped screaming only when she realized that she could no longer hear the skunk man's feet pounding on the stairs behind her. It was suddenly quiet. Too quiet. She could hear her heart beating. It felt like it was going to come out through her nostrils. She saw the glowing red "Exit" sign directly above her head and the number "3" next to it. She was almost to the lobby level! Her screams had driven the skunk man away!

Liffey could hardly breathe now. Her asthma was making her chest tight with the struggle to get enough air into her lungs. She had not used her emergency inhaler all day and had probably done more breathing running down these stairs today than she had done in the entire last year. She was panting and gasping but determined to reach the safety of the lobby. If this chase was going to have a happy ending, she needed to get *out* of this stairwell and back into safe surroundings!

She choked back tears as she thought how misled she had been by the pretty redheaded lady who had seemed so nice. *How* could that friendly face have been on someone who was obviously working with that *awful* man? Liffey's father had often told her that looks can be deceiving. She knew now that he was right.

"Just two more floors to the lobby. I *can* do it! I *will* do it!"

Liffey doubted that the skunk man would be able to beat her to the lobby if he were waiting for an elevator after he left the stairwell. Besides, he would not want to confront her in the lobby. He had hoped to catch her in the stairwell where she would have been easy prey.

Liffey resumed her flight down the stairs at a slower pace now, working hard to get enough air into her lungs. She could not stop thinking about where the shopping bag and doll would be by now. Probably in one of the expensive suites on the 6th floor where the skunk man and redhead were now laughing together about how they had outsmarted her and practically scared her to death.

Had the skunk man and his redheaded accomplice beaten her after all? Liffey feared that the sparkling solo dress crown was *gone* for good and that now she would never know the story it could have told her. No one would *ever* believe her theory about stolen jewels and her father would be so angry with her when Louise told him she had "lost" Liffey, that she would probably never be able to go to another feis again without her Aunt Jean or father along as watch dogs. She had *really* done it this time!!

When Liffey finally reached the "Lobby Exit" door in the stairwell, a hotel manager who was posted there, asked her if she had heard anyone screaming in the stairwell. Liffey considered admitting that it was she who had been screaming while trying to escape from the skunk man but was too weary to go into the whole thing. She shook her head "no" and headed for the lobby and one of its big, soft chairs.

Liffey was fighting back tears and making little gurgling noises as she continued the struggle to get enough air into her lungs. At least she had avoided Louise, Liffey thought. Although she *had* to admit that she would not mind riding in that wheelchair now! Her feet were throbbing and her legs felt weak and rubbery like after running the mile at school. Looking around for a place to collapse, she spotted an empty chair not too far from the main entrance to the hotel lobby and gratefully sank down into it.

Liffey leaned back and felt the comfortable softness of the chair. Then she felt the tears that were running down her face and pooling at the neckline of her uncomfortable dance dress. She licked the biggest ones away and brushed a few smaller ones away with her hands. She concentrated on her breathing which was improving now that she was no longer running down the stairs like a maniac.

After this last chase with the skunk man, Liffey realized she might have been in more danger than she could have ever imagined when she chose to follow a doll with a crown around in a hotel. She had been pursued *three* times now by the skunk man. What in the world did he think she knew? Why would he think a thirteen-year-old girl in an Irish dancer's costume was a threat? Was he actually trying to hurt her or just scare her away?

It was like they could read each other's minds. Liffey *knew* that he *knew* that she *knew* that the jewels were real. But so what? Why should he *care*? Who would even *believe* her if she started telling a story about a solo dress crown being used to smuggle jewels?

Apparently, thought Liffey, the skunk man did not want to take any chances.

# CHAPTER SEVENTEEN
## Collapse

Although Liffey was not sure she could even move now, let alone dance, she remembered she *was* at a feis and was supposed to be *dancing*. Should she change into her hard shoes and try to do a Hornpipe, or get up and try to get through the Treble Jig? Surely it had to be time to do the hard shoe steps by now?

She would have to go back to the Jig stage to find her dance bag and get her hard shoes. She knew she would not place even if she did somehow manage to get to a Treble Jig or Hornpipe stage, unless the judge gave her points for breathing! On the other hand, if she did *not* do another dance step, her father would cross-examine her endlessly as to why she had gone all the way to St. Louis and had only done one step.

Liffey wondered if she could stand up. She looked down at her waist and saw that her number was still tied to it with the long piece of string from her registration packet. Liffey had almost forgotten why she was at this hotel in the first place. It seemed like a million years ago that she had found herself lying on the Jig stage floor.

How much time had passed? Liffey had absolutely no idea, but it seemed like a lifetime. As she struggled with the idea of getting up and actually trying to *walk* again, she studied the front desk trying to see if Louise was somewhere behind it.

Louise did not appear to be anywhere in the vicinity of the

front desk or lobby. "Great," thought Liffey, "I cannot think of any good reason to explain why I ditched the paramedics. I will have to avoid her until I can get out of here and get to the airport."

Liffey was scheduled to fly out of St. Louis and back to Chicago that night after the feis was over on a 9:00 p.m. plane. She fervently hoped that Louise would not tell her father that she had dumped her and fled. That could mean Aunt Jean for the next feis, and Liffey was not sure which she feared most, fleeing from the slimy skunk man, or dancing on a competition stage with her deranged aunt watching, ready to burst out with the "Kick em High, Kick em Low, Liffey, Liffey, GO, GO, GO!" cheer. It was almost a tie.

# CHAPTER EIGHTEEN
## The Smell of a Skunk

Taking full advantage of the much needed rest the lobby was providing, Liffey burrowed down into the comfortable chair and began to drift off. She was almost asleep when the creepy crawly pins and needles started again. Startled awake by them, she tried to sink even further down in the chair so she would not be noticed by the skunk man or redhead. Liffey was certain they were close by.

There was quite a crowd standing near her chair because the results board was in the Mississippi Room, right off the lobby. It was noisy in there. Dancers and musicians and singers and parents were all standing around waiting for their competition results to be posted on long strips of cardboard tacked to the wall. Liffey studied the throng of waiting people and was almost relieved she did not have to be in there right now waiting for the "Place" boxes to be filled in with what usually turned out to be other dancers' numbers.

The skunk man was very close now. Liffey could *feel* him. But this time, Liffey knew she was safe. She was sitting in a big chair in a lobby full of little girls switching from ghillies into their hard shoes. There was nothing the skunk man could do to her here, so Liffey waited and watched the front desk and the bank of elevators.

She did not have to wait long. There they were. *Together*! The redheaded woman was still carrying the shopping bag and was now also wheeling a small suitcase behind her as she walked briskly through the lobby with the skunk man. They stopped. They were within three feet of Liffey's chair. She could smell the redhead's perfume.

Liffey watched with disgust as the redhead placed a little kiss on the skunk man's left cheek. "Yuk!" Liffey muttered under her breath. "She's the skunk man's *girlfriend?*" Neither one of them noticed her sitting there, sinking down as far as she could into the oversized lobby chair. Her father had always said that girls wearing Irish dance wigs all looked alike. She was relieved now to find out that he was apparently right.

Liffey's attention was drawn to the tiny, sparkling rainbows that were bouncing up and down the redheaded lady's fingers and right arm. The doll's crown, which Liffey could not see from her chair, must have been reflecting light from the huge light fixture that was directly above the skunk man and his accomplice. The little dancing rainbows activated the solo dress side of Liffey's brain and she felt a solo dress trance starting again even in the midst of danger. She had to *force* herself not to think about her own future solo dress and crown. Not now. She needed to do something about *this* crown! Right now! Right here! But what?

She knew she only had a few seconds because it was obvious that the redhead was leaving. The redhead had actually *kissed* the skunk man good-bye! Liffey shuddered again. That kiss was definitely Halloween material.

"Good luck," Liffey heard the skunk man say to his girlfriend. "Thanks for meeting me in St. Looey," he went on in the same creepy, raspy voice Liffey had heard when she had fallen in the ballroom. The redhead giggled.

"Sick!" Liffey cringed, knowing that she now had only a matter of seconds to deal with the impending departure of the redheaded lady who had actually *kissed* the skunk man. *Why* was she leaving without him? "Is the skunk man staying behind to continue looking for *me?*" Liffey groaned. She did not think she had enough energy left in her to be chased around the hotel again. Her arms and legs felt like lead.

The redheaded lady began walking away from the skunk man towards the main exit doors of the hotel lobby. *Another* now or never moment like the old Elvis song her father was always singing in the shower. Liffey decided that in the past twenty-four hours, she had had enough now or never moments for a lifetime. But if she did not do something right *now*, she knew she would *never* know for certain whether the sparkling solo dress crown's diamonds were real and why she had been chased all over the hotel by the sinister skunk man.

# CHAPTER NINETEEN
## The Thinking Cap

Liffey gathered all her strength, put her thinking cap back on her head, and considered her options. Then she jumped up directly in *front* of the skunk man who was watching his redheaded friend approach the lobby doors. He had obviously not seen Liffey buried in the big lounge chair watching him being kissed. Face to face now, Liffey saw the startled look on his face.

Slowly, the skunk man's look of surprise morphed into a smug sneer as if to say, "Too bad! I guess this is how it ends. What are you going to do *now*, little Irish dancer girl?" He looked away from Liffey.

The skunk man craned his neck, watching his girlfriend make her way through the crowded lobby towards the main hotel exit. Liffey could see that there was quite a group waiting outside by the taxi stand. His girlfriend would have to wait her turn unless she could somehow figure out how to get to the front of the long taxi loading line.

As the skunk man looked nervously out through the main lobby doors, deliberately avoiding Liffey's eyes, she took a deep breath, like the ones she took before beginning a dance step competition. Then she started screaming again at the top of her lungs! She was very relieved to discover she did actually have enough breath left in her to scream again because everything depended on it!

The skunk man appeared to be very unnerved by her screams and peered around the lobby apprehensively at the growing crowd, still making no eye contact with Liffey. The redheaded lady, who had not quite made it out of the hotel lobby yet, came to a halt right in front of the lobby's revolving doors, not daring to turn around and look. Then she was moving again and disappeared through the twirling doors.

Liffey knew it was time for her plan to move into high gear, so she pointed towards the revolving doors and shouted: "Give me back my doll! You *stole* it! It's *my* doll! *Help! She stole my doll!*"

The look of shock and dismay on the skunk man's face gave Liffey a surge of confidence as she turned away from him and ran after the redhead who was now outside the lobby doors frantically hailing a cab.

Liffey raced outside through the revolving doors just as a uniformed policeman, who was directing the heavy traffic in the hotel's no parking lanes, stepped in front of the redhead, preventing her from opening the door of the taxi she had pushed in front of everybody else to get. In a calm voice, the officer asked the redhead if she would please step aside to discuss the little girl's accusation before she left the hotel grounds.

Liffey ran up to the policeman as he was escorting the redhead back into the lobby. Frantically, Liffey told him her theory that she was *sure* that this doll's crown had *stolen* jewels in it and that the redheaded lady and the skunk man *had* to be stopped! Liffey turned around to point out the skunk man to the officer only to find that he had vanished! With a sinking feeling, Liffey realized that she looked ridiculous.

The policeman and the redheaded woman were exchanging grownup "what a bunch of nonsense" looks as Liffey heard herself babbling incoherently trying to explain what she had been through in the last twenty-four hours.

"Find him! You *have* to *find* him!" Liffey said to the policeman who was giving the redhead a "You can go now look."

Liffey continued, "The skunk man *knows* that I *know* that he *knows* that I *know*, and he's *after* me!"

"There, there. Calm down young lady. We'll sort this out. Do you have a receipt for this doll, Miss?" the policeman asked the redhead in a business-like manner. Liffey groaned audibly as she watched the redhead take a small piece of paper out of the bag and hand it to the policeman. He studied it carefully and then said aloud: "One porcelain Irish Dancer doll: $59.65."

The policeman exhaled and told the redhead she was free to leave the hotel with the doll. With a pitying look at Liffey, the redhead turned, walked out the doors, and entered another waiting cab.

# CHAPTER TWENTY
## Lost in the Fog

By this time, there were over a hundred curious Irish dancers and their parents watching the Liffey "reality show." The policeman gently took Liffey's limp hand and said, "Come, dear. I'm Officer Gibbons. Let's find your parents and sort this out."

"I don't *have* a mother and my father is in Chicago and you let them get *away!*" Liffey choked through her tears, struggling to breathe.

Officer Gibbons, alarmed at Liffey's obvious breathing difficulty and her ashen skin color, talked into his radio. He then carefully picked up Liffey, who was too weak to resist, and carried her through the crowd to the closest couch.

"Move aside, please," he directed the crowd, "We have a medical emergency here." He placed her down gently, propping her head up with a pillow handed to him by an alert concierge. Officer Gibbons continued to hold her trembling hand and asked for a blanket.

Liffey began sobbing inconsolably which made her breathing even more labored. Alarmed by Liffey's deteriorating appearance, Officer Gibbons talked into his radio again just as the EMTs arrived with the same stretcher and now, an oxygen tank. "Oh no," thought Liffey. Now I have *totally* messed up."

"*Here* you are!" one of the white coats exclaimed! "*Where* have you been? We have been looking everywhere for this girl," they explained to Officer Gibbons.

Officer Gibbons looked puzzled and continued talking into his radio. "We need to take her to ER," one of the white coats was saying. "She fainted earlier today and then she bolted when we answered another call."

"Do you have an emergency inhaler?" one of the voices asked. Liffey could not answer. She was shaking all over and working too hard to breathe to even cry anymore. She was sure that she was going to be in more trouble now than she could have *ever* imagined. She nodded faintly and before she could explain that the inhaler was in her dance bag which was still at the U-13 Jig stage, she felt herself slipping into a foggy place where all the faces around her belonged to the skunk man, except for the twins. There they were again, standing on top of a mountain this time. They were smiling and waving and holding their trophies up higher and higher. Far away she heard a voice saying: "200ccs *now!*" It sounded like her father's voice, and it was a command, not a suggestion.

Liffey was jolted out of the foggy place right back into the center of the hotel lobby with all its curious, staring faces, and realized that she was sitting up now and looking at Louise who appeared to be very worried and concerned.

Someone was lifting her again. "No, it can't be," thought Liffey. She was still dreaming. Or was she? She collapsed into the embracing arms of Robert Rivers and smelled the familiar aftershave he always wore. She pressed her wet cheek against his face knowing she was safe at last. "Daddy!" gasped Liffey, "thank *goodness* you are here."

"I will take her for an MRI myself," Robert Rivers told Louise and the paramedics. Officer Gibbons said that he would cancel the ambulance he had just called and guide them to the nearest emergency room.

Liffey struggled to get words out of her mouth. She tried

to tell her father that she needed him to get someone to *stop* the redheaded lady before she got away with the jewels. But it was hard to talk in sentences. She heard little croaking noises coming out of her throat when she tried to speak.

Robert Rivers carried Liffey through the hotel doors into the waiting limousine he had hired at the airport. Carefully, he placed Liffey on the wide backseat and covered her with a blanket, gently propping her wigged head up with several velvet pillows.

# CHAPTER TWENTY-ONE
## Chasing the Crown

L iffey knew she had to persuade her father to take immediate action or the diamond solo dress crown would vanish forever with the redheaded lady. Officer Gibbons told Robert Rivers about Liffey's diamond crown theory and also her account of having been chased around the hotel by a man who looked like a skunk. Even Liffey had to admit that the whole thing sounded absurd when she listened to someone else telling the story!

The little bit of rest Liffey had been able to get since the wild chase down the stairwell seemed to have restored her vocal chords and she was very relieved now to hear actual words coming out of her mouth instead of croaks as the limo started off for the hospital.

"Daddy, I am *not* crazy! There *really* is a redheaded woman who led me into a trap and I really *was* chased by a man who looks like a skunk." Liffey continued: "He chased me even *before* I fell on the stage this morning. I *know* that they are carrying around a doll wearing a crown of *real* diamonds."

"The diamonds looked just like the ones I saw at the Tower of London when I was ten-years-old. Remember when I got into trouble at the Tower because I kept riding the people mover past them over and over?"

\*\*\*

Robert Rivers smiled, recalling how difficult it had been to get Liffey to leave the crown jewels that day. Her sitter had called him out of a meeting to "negotiate" terms with Liffey so she would voluntarily leave the Tower grounds. Liffey had asked her father if she could just borrow or rent some of the crowns so she could put on a play at home about all of the queens who had worn them. He had told her he would look into it.

*** 

But now, Liffey was *insisting* that these diamonds were far too big for a little crown on a doll's head and that they sparkled just like the ones in Queen Victoria's crowns. Liffey was very relieved to note that her father did not have one of those stupid adult smiles on his face as he listened intently to her description of the events of the last twenty-four hours. He did not even lecture or threaten her with Aunt Jean.

"Liffey," her father began gently, "I have left you alone too often by yourself. No wonder you live in such a cloak and dagger world. I am not going to be so busy anymore. I am going to spend more time with you," he said, clasping her tiny hands in his, as the limo followed Officer Gibbons to the hospital.

"Daddy," Liffey was firm this time and something in her voice made her father listen to her in a more attentive way. "Daddy, I had those pins and needle feelings around the skunk man *all* the time. Even *before* I would actually even see him! You *know* I never get those unless I am in danger. *You know* how it works! Please *do* something, Daddy!" Liffey pleaded.

They pulled into the Emergency Room driveway behind Officer Gibbons' squad car, and were met by hospital staff who insisted Liffey enter the hospital in a wheelchair. She pressed her father's hand to her face. He told her he would follow her in after he spoke briefly with Officer Gibbons. The conversation between the lawyer and the police officer was short and to the point. Robert Rivers then returned to the limo and spoke into his cell phone as Officer Gibbons called the police dispatcher from his squad car radio. The two men ended their conversations at the same moment and Mr. Rivers thanked Officer Gibbons for his help. Officer Gibbons jumped into his police car and told Mr. Rivers he would report back to him within the hour. Then he turned on his siren and raced off.

***

Liffey discovered that she could finally breathe again, so she resumed her crying as she waited on the examination table in the ugly ER room. Liffey wept *big* tears of humiliation and rage. How *could* she have let things get so *totally* out of control? *Nobody* believed her and now her father would think she was either insane or untrustworthy—or both. And to put the icing on the despair cake, the awful skunk man *and* redheaded lady *and* sparkling solo dress crown were on their way now to some unknown place for some unknown purpose. "I am an *idiot*," Liffey squeaked out feebly to herself.

"Where *was* her father?" Liffey frowned. "And *where* was the hospital staff?" It seemed like she had been dumped here alone on this cold table forever. Eventually, a doctor and nurse walked in to "triage" her. Liffey was far too mentally exhausted to ask what in the world "triage" meant and tried to politely answer their questions as to the events of the longest day in the history of mankind.

"Yes," she probably had fainted. "No," she did not think she had ever fainted before. "Yes," she had asthma. "No," she was not sick. "No, no. Yes, yes. No," and on and on. Liffey was not even listening to their questions anymore. She could not stop thinking about the crown and the sparkling diamonds and the redheaded woman and the creepy skunk man. She felt herself trembling again. She needed to get *out* of this triage thing and find the redhead! She would have to bolt and sneak back to the limo. And since the doctor and nurse were not looking and seemed to be very busy writing notes about her condition, she looked around the triage room for a way out.

*\*\*\**

But before she had begun her escape, Robert Rivers finally appeared in the triage doorway with an enormous grin on his face. He flashed Liffey the victory sign which made her think she *had* to be *hallucinating*. She had always wondered what "going over the edge" meant. *This* must be it! She must *be* there now. Why else would her father look so happy and *pleased* with her? Liffey had never even imagined causing so much commotion. She had outdone herself this time! But here was her father, smiling proudly at her and walking over to the examination table. Liffey could not come up with any good reason why he suddenly looked relieved and happy instead of weary and concerned.

# CHAPTER TWENTY-TWO
## Conflict Diamonds

L iffey," began her father, "I am *very* sorry I left you alone in here for such a long time. But I knew you would want me to follow up on your redheaded lady with the shopping bag doll."

"Daddy, *what* did you find out?" Liffey fairly shrieked. The triage staff politely stood up and left the room with their assessment charts, leaving Liffey alone with her father.

"Well, Liffey," he continued, "I made several phone calls to a police detective I had worked with a few years ago in Chicago on a murder trial. I told her about your stolen diamond theory. I did not mention your warning feelings, because professional investigators like facts, not feelings. But I *did* discuss the fact that that you were seriously frightened by a man at the hotel, and that he needed to be questioned and perhaps detained for his behavior. I also said that there was a redheaded woman carrying a shopping bag containing an Irish dancer doll with a diamond crown, probably headed for the airport, and that she needed to be questioned as to the whereabouts of the man who had been chasing you."

Robert Rivers went on: "Apparently, a squad car was dispatched to the airport and the officers found the redhead checking in at a flight to London counter in the International Terminal. Officer Gibbons was there too, to identify her, since he had seen her at the hotel. Then, when the police walked up to her, she began acting suspiciously. She panicked and began running away from them!"

"Naturally, the police pursued her. When they apprehended her, they took her to airport customs security who thought that the jewels in the crown looked suspicious, just like you did. But before they even started questioning her, she began crying and said she did not know why she had allowed herself to get involved with her diamond-smuggling boyfriend because *she* was the one who always took all the risks trying to sneak them in and out of countries. She was taken into custody and there are some federal agents on the way right now to take over the investigation."

"So the jewels *were* real? I *knew* it. I *knew* it!" squealed Liffey, doing a little victory dance. "The jewels *were* real," Mr. Rivers smiled. "But where were they going?" inquired Liffey. "What would make someone risk going to jail carrying around stolen diamonds like that? Why not just sell them to a jeweler or diamond trader?" Liffey asked.

"Well," Mr. Rivers speculated, "Those diamonds probably came from a part of the world where no one wanted a money trail left behind. I remember reading recently about revolutionaries in some countries who use diamonds to pay for overthrowing their governments. They are called 'conflict diamonds,' I think."

"Conflict diamonds?" asked Liffey. "Yes," Robert Rivers went on to explain. "Some third world countries have large diamond mining companies. Sometimes it is not too difficult to bribe corrupt company officials to allow some of the diamonds to 'disappear' during the mining process. And it can get even more complicated than that. Sometimes rebel armies in diamond mining countries take over the mines, mine the diamonds themselves, and then somehow smuggle the uncut stones out of the country. Then the rough diamonds are cut and polished by professionals. Mostly in India, I think, although Belgium and Amsterdam also have large operations. Terrorists and money launderers are often involved in diamond smuggling. It is *big, big* money and your skunk man has to be working for some kind of criminal organization!"

Robert Rivers shivered a little as he contemplated how fortunate his daughter had been to have escaped the clutches of an international jewel thief!

"The diamonds finally end up in underground smuggling channels to get them into countries where there are dishonest jewelers who will pay large amounts of money without any questions asked."

"And finally," her father concluded, "The money is used to buy guns and equipment to finance 'conflicts,' which is another word for a war, in third world countries, or to pay for terrorist activities. It is an ugly business."

"Your redheaded lady was probably transporting conflict diamonds that had already been polished out of the country! Your skunk man was probably supposed to meet her in Belgium or London or maybe Amsterdam and then complete the smuggling job himself. He needed an innocent looking courier to get them in and out of the country. The diamond solo dress crown was a clever idea. And *you* figured it out, Liffey! My little girl! I am so proud of you!"

Liffey was speechless. It seemed that she had actually prevented a really big crime and maybe even a *war* all because she had noticed that the skunk man was always turning up at dance competitions and she thought he had seemed out of place!

If she had not followed him onto the elevator and noticed the diamonds on the solo dress crown, they would probably be out of the country by now and headed to a jeweler for money to pay for weapons. "If only I had followed him *before* this feis," thought Liffey, trying to remember how many times she had seen him at other feiseanna. She was concerned that perhaps wars were already being fought with the money from other conflict diamonds the skunk man had smuggled.

Liffey threw herself into her father's arms. "Let's get out of here, Daddy. I am *fine!*" Robert Rivers agreed that Liffey seemed to be breathing and acting normally again and signed the hospital release forms. He smiled proudly as Liffey did leap overs and hop 1-2-3s out to the limousine.

Driving away from the hospital, Liffey leaned her head on her father's comforting shoulder and thought again about the redheaded lady. Her father had told her the lady had panicked at the airport. That probably meant she was not an experienced, professional thief like the skunk man. For some reason, that made Liffey feel a little better. Liffey thought that she had seemed too nice to be associated with the horrible skunk man. But she *had* kissed him!

Liffey shuddered again remembering how totally grossed out she had been when she had witnessed the kiss in the hotel lobby.

# CHAPTER TWENTY-THREE
## The Messipi

A s the limo passed by the St. Louis Arch, Liffey begged her father to stop so they could go to the top of the Arch and get a good look at the Mississippi. She knew her father had flown to St. Louis on the law firm's private jet, so there would be no plane they had to catch tonight at the airport where the redheaded lady was probably now being questioned. Liffey also knew her father was a *total* sucker for historical things and places, so she added, "What could be *more historical* than the St. Louis Arch, Daddy?" Liffey was thrilled when her father agreed and asked the limo driver to turn around and park at the big museum located next to the Arch.

*This time*, Liffey was only too happy to have someone with her as she and her father stepped out of the limo to explore. *This* time, she would be only too happy to ask *permission* from her father to do absolutely anything at all. Even permission to speak! Liffey tried not to think about the skunk man again and how he had chased her. She had *never* been that frightened before!

Had the police found him yet? It was hard to relax thinking that *he* was out there somewhere. But now she was with her father and he would protect her from *anyone* and *anything.*

The museum was interesting with its Native American artifacts and Lewis and Clark and river boat exhibits, but Liffey was impatient to get to the top of the Arch that she had been looking at from her hotel window for the past two days. Her father bought the tickets for the tram ride up and they got into a short line to wait for a tram carrying passengers on the north leg of the Arch.

Since they had been told that both trams were operating today, they planned to come back down the Arch on its south leg. Studying the brochure he was handed when he bought the tram tickets, Robert Rivers began giving Liffey facts and figures about the Arch they were about to enter.

"Oh no," groaned Liffey. In her excitement to get up into the Arch, she had forgotten how her father always launched into his historian brain when they would visit historical places of interest together. Sometimes she really enjoyed the facts that he threw at her like fast pitches, but now he was telling her how the Arch was actually designed and built.

"It is a catenary curve, Liffey, and it is 630 feet high." Liffey feared her father might go into what kind of math was involved with a catenary curve and she was far too mentally exhausted to learn the catenary curve equation today. Quickly, Liffey told him she had not studied enough geometry to discuss a complicated curve equation. Her father bought it and went back to reading the brochure.

Liffey could hear the tram coming. She tried to visualize

how the tram could get *up* the Arch. Surely it would not be on tracks like the incline she had once ridden in Pittsburgh straight up the side of a steep hill? That would be *way* too scary. Like an incredible new ride designed for Disney World or something. Then she saw eight small capsules that had to be the "tram" arriving at the loading area. The capsules reminded Liffey of the purple discus inhaler she used to control her asthma. They were almost round! "This will be *great*," thought Liffey, as she and her father stepped into one of the capsules by themselves. The other seats remained empty as their capsule started its ride up to the top of the Arch.

Since they were the only tram riders, Robert Rivers continued his lecture. "On clear days, Liffey, you can see for thirty miles! And we are going up sixty-three stories high!" Now things got *really* boring but Liffey was stuck in the capsule with her inquisitive father.

"There are 1,076 stairs leading up to the top. But only maintenance crews are permitted to use them." Liffey was not really listening to her father's facts anymore and would probably regret it later when he would inevitably quiz her.

These capsules reminded Liffey of something. "I know! They look like the barrels on cement mixing trucks!" Liffey was impressed that she made that connection considering she knew nothing at all about cement trucks. Except that they were noisy. This ride was fairly noisy too. There were lots of motor sounds and clicking. But not nearly as scary as Liffey had initially feared the ride would be. Then they were there! The very top of the Gateway to the West!

Robert Rivers looked at his watch and announced that the ride had taken approximately four minutes. Liffey nodded at him as she hopped off the tram and ran to the long, narrow window in the long, narrow viewing area.

Liffey looked down at the Mississippi River and the City of St. Louis. She tried with all her might to see Tom Sawyer and Huck Finn drifting along on their raft. But they were not there. She could not see them. There was just the river.

"Look, Daddy!" Liffey pointed to a paddle wheel river boat which was churning up so much water that it looked like a water spout. "Maybe we could come back next year and do the boat trip?" she asked hopefully.

But before her father could answer, a wave of sadness came over Liffey, as she realized that nothing would ever be quite the same again. Things would be different now. She looked down at the river and understood what it was her father had tried so hard to shield her from. Her collision with the skunk man and redheaded woman had taken something precious away from her. She could almost see some of her childhood floating away on the Father of Waters far below.

Liffey also *knew* that the skunk man *knew* that she *knew* he was still out there and that he had escaped. She also knew that they would meet again one day and the next time, she would be ready for him. She would NEVER put herself in harm's way again.

# CHAPTER TWENTY-FOUR
## Results

The Rivers' limousine maneuvered into the V.I.P. parking slot reserved for guests who had booked a suite on the 6th floor. Liffey gave her father an inquisitive look and he responded: "You *are* a V.I.P., Liffey! *We* are staying in Suite 600 tonight! We will order Chinese and watch movies and then *you* will sleep. You can give me all the details tomorrow. Tonight you will relax and eat shrimp fried rice. You saved someone millions of dollars today when you solved the mystery of the sparkling solo dress crown. We will send *them* the bill when we find out who they are!"

Robert and Liffey Rivers strolled arm in arm together into the crowded hotel lobby which was still packed with clumps of dancers and their entourages. This time the stares Liffey received were obvious. No one even *pretended* not to look at her as she proudly walked with her father over to the hotel registration desk!

Liffey put a genuine smile back on her face as they approached the hotel desk where Mr. Rivers asked if they could have the room key to move Liffey's belongings up to the 6th floor.

"Where was Louise?" wondered Liffey. Maybe she was off duty by now. "Daddy," Liffey began, "may I look for Louise to apologize for all the hassles I caused her today before we go upstairs?" Liffey thought Louise might be bringing a luggage cart up to a room.

"Liffey," smiled Mr. Rivers, "Louise is not here at the moment." "Oh well," Liffey sighed, wondering *how* he knew that. But then, her father always seemed to know everything! "I just wanted to say I was sorry that I gave her such a run around. She really was very nice and I did not mean to cause so much trouble. Maybe I will leave a note for her here at the desk."

"Liffey," Mr. Rivers said, "Louise does not work here." "What?" Liffey was confused. "What do you mean she doesn't work here? She wears a concierge uniform and knows her way around the hotel."

"Louise is a private detective, Liffey," her father said, smiling again. Liffey was stunned. "*She* is the police detective I called about going to the airport and questioning the redheaded woman. She works as a private investigator when she is not on duty with the police force."

"*Louise?*"

Liffey could hardly believe it.

"Louise is a detective?"

"You hired a *private investigator* to *follow* me around the hotel?"

"Liffey," Mr. Rivers explained patiently, "there are state laws about minors checking into hotels. The only way this hotel and all the others would accept you as a guest, was if I hired an adult, Louise in this case, to be responsible for you. She stayed in the room next to yours and kept a log of your comings and goings for me. Besides, you do not think I would allow you to check into an out-of-state hotel all by yourself, do you?"

Liffey had no ready answer for her father. She was too tired to think about anything anymore except a soft pillow and the comfortable suite of rooms waiting for her on the *6th floor!*

And shrimp fried rice!

On the way to the elevators that always took at least ten minutes to come, Liffey and Robert Rivers passed the feis results room.

"Liffey, you danced the Jig today, didn't you? Let's check the results."

"Daddy, I *passed out* right after my Jig. I really don't think the judges here give *sympathy* places."

"But you *did* finish it, right?" he went on. "Yes, I guess so," Liffey answered softly, trying to remember if she actually had finished the Jig.

"Well, let's just check and see. You still have your number on. What competition number was it?"

"Number J-25, I think," Liffey replied absently.

Liffey did not even bother going over to look at the results board with her father. Instead, she walked over to take her place at the bank of elevators.

She could only hope that her next feis went a little more smoothly and that there would be only the excitement of the results board to occupy her the next time she danced. She was trying to recall the concierges at all the other hotels where she had stayed "alone." They must have been detectives too!

When her father returned a moment later, his face did

not show any good fortune news, so Liffey went back to her thoughts about the skunk man and what he might have done after the redheaded woman left.

Was he still in the hotel? Since Louise was a police detective, she would be following up on that. Still, it would be nice to know if the skunk man had been apprehended.

What about the shoe vendor? Was he too part of the plot?

Had Louise entered the stairwell and scared off the skunk man? Or did Liffey's screams drive the skunk man away? Liffey's head was clouded with questions without answers.

Liffey slipped her hand into her father's. Robert Rivers' eyes were filled with tears as he leaned down to put a little kiss on Liffey's forehead. She felt one of them running down her face like one of the dew drops from the May lilacs at home. "I guess he doesn't want to break the bad news," Liffey thought.

Then her father cleared his throat and began to speak in a husky voice that Liffey had never heard before. "I wonder, Ms. Rivers, what was the color of your mother's first solo dress?"

Liffey had thought about that too. There was only one Irish dancer photo of her mother as a young girl, and it showed her in a school costume, not her solo dress.

But now, her father was giving Liffey one of his expectant "fill-in-the-blanks" looks with his hands waving around doing a kind of Charades "sounds like" gesture.

And then Liffey *knew*. She *knew* that her father *knew* that she already *knew* the best news in the entire world! *"I GOT A FIRST PLACE! I GOT A FIRST!!!"*

The broad smile on Robert Rivers' face told her that she had indeed earned her solo dress today. Liffey Rivers, the girl who always noticed the little things that most people just walked right by, had not seen her *own number* on the results board that day in the "1st Place" box!

She squeezed her father's hand tightly as they entered the almost empty elevator. She would pick up her first *gold* medal later. After the shrimp fried rice.

Liffey closed her eyes. There were the twins again with their black hair shining under the blue stage lights.

And there *she* was, standing arm in arm with a twin on either side of her this time. They were equals now!

All three solo dress crowns sparkled and dazzled the beholders like prisms reflecting the rising sun!

*The End*

# LIFFEY'S LINGO:

**Feis:** A feis is an Irish competition. It sounds like "fesh." They are fun if you place. Sometimes even if you don't place, you can be happy for someone else who *did* place, especially if they are totally freaked out when they don't expect to place and then do (place).

**Feiseanna:** This means more than one feis. Like: "I went to lots of feiseanna last summer." This was the name of my imaginary friend, "Feshanna," joke that Bert did not get.

**Ceili:** Ceili is another Irish word. It is a group dance. Figure dances are ceili dances. It sounds like "kaylee."

**Hop 1, 2, 3s:** This is my favorite step because it is sooo easy! It's almost like skipping.

**Ghillies:** They are kind of like ballet slippers and they lace up with really, really long shoe laces.

**Adjudicators:** They are the feis judges who never give me a first place in any of my Novice steps.

**Drillers:** They are older dancers who help teach. Some are great but some have favorite students and give them all their attention.

**Solo dress crown:** I have to have one! Mine will be incredible! It will match my solo dress.

**Solo dress:** At my school, it is what you get when you win a first place in a Novice step at a feis. Or, if you get chosen and sent to an oireachtas *before* you win a 1st place in Novice at a feis. But you have to wear one at an oireachtas if you get to do solo steps there (I think). So if you get picked to go to an oireachtas, you get a solo dress, even if you didn't get a 1st place at a feis. I think.

**Oireachtas:** Too hard to explain. It's a really big deal for dancers who get to go to it. Everybody picked for one seems way too nervous before them. Like they are going to flunk all their final exams or something and not get promoted to the 9th grade. It sounds like "oh-rock-tus." Oh—and if dancers do not get a "recall" at it, they are totally freaked out so do NOT ask them anything about it. Pretend it never happened. I am serious.

**Trip to the Cottage:** This is a figure dance ceili. The name is a *total* jinx. Don't do it! Tell your teacher to find some other figure dance! There are lots of other ones! Tell them to learn another one and teach it to you.

**Jig:** The very first step you learn in Irish dancing. You spend a whole year doing it, so you better like it! It is my favorite step because I do not have to remember too many things when I do it.

**Hornpipe:** You wear your hard shoes for this dance. It is set in 2/4 or 4/4 time. Be sure to make a lot of noise when you do it! Pound the floor as hard as you can! Hold your breath only when necessary! Or, you could make an Arch crown to distract the judges if you are in St. Louis. If you are at a feis somewhere else, the Arch crown probably would not work too well. But you can use your imagination! Like: A bridge crown if you are in San Francisco. A cheese crown if you are dancing in Wisconsin. But not an ugly one like the Green Bay Packer fans wear. Or, if you are in Seattle, you could do that space needle thing. Lots of states have mountains…a mountain crown might work. Washington D.C. dancers could make national monument solo dress crowns. And, if you made a Lincoln Memorial crown, you could also use it in Illinois. The idea is to have the adjudicators focusing on your crown, not your feet.

a/k/a: This means "also known as."

Celtic: There were ancient tribes of Celts all over Europe. Lots of them ended up in Ireland. Celtic is a word that means "of the Celts," like Celtic jewelry and artifacts (really old stuff).

U-13: You dance in this group if you were 12-years-old on January 1st of last year! The "U" means you were under 13-years-old then.

Treble Jig: It is a hard shoe dance that is a bit faster and peppier than the Hornpipe. I like it.

Queen Maeve: She was like Wonder Woman. She took an army to Ulster to steal the Brown Bull of Cooley. And she got it! She is buried on top of a huge mountain in her armor and anybody (it is an easy walk) can climb up it and then see all over County Sligo and even into County Donegal. Her grave has a 50-foot pile of stones on it (called a cairn) that you can climb on when you get to the top of the mountain.

**Book of Kells:** Kells is a place in Ireland. Monks copied the Gospels at their monastery in Iona and for some reason, their work ended up in a monastery at Kells—maybe to protect it. Today, the manuscripts are kept at Trinity College in Dublin in a glass case so they don't crumble up and deteriorate.

**Knocknarea:** This is the huge mountain in County Sligo where Queen Maeve is buried on top. It has a red glow behind it at night that could be fairy light! Nobody has bothered to excavate her cairn (tomb) to see if Maeve is really still in there because it would cost way too much money or something.

**Nationals:** These are really big competitions in the U.S. Dancers from other countries can enter the U.S. Nationals too. I am not ready for them.

**Slip Jig:** My favorite step. It is an all-girl dance and requires lots of grace (and energy). If you do ballet, you will like it.

**Reel:** A soft shoe dance that is faster than the Slip Jig. I don't like it very much because it makes me feel like a grasshopper.

**Tower of London Ravens:** These birds sort of look like crows. They hang around the Tower Green because their wings get clipped so that they cannot fly away. They have always been at the Tower. If I could get a baby bird Raven, I would not clip its wings and then I could train it to be like a carrier pigeon and send notes to my father. Some Ravens can talk, I think, so I could train mine to do that so I would have someone to talk to.

# AUNT JEAN'S FEIS CHEERS

## Untitled

Kick em HIGH!! Kick em Low!!

Liffey, Liffey, GO! GO! GO!

## CEILI DANCE CHEER

The team is in a huddle!
(echo) The team is in a huddle!

The captain lowers his/her head!
(echo) The captain lowers his/her head!

They all got together!
(echo) They all got together!
And this is what they said!
The team is red hot!
The team is red hot!
The team is red hot!
BURN EM UP!!!

# TIN CAN CEILI CHEER

Sittin in a feis stand beatin on a tin can
Who can?
We can!
Nobody else can!
B-E-A-T-Beat-em-Beat-em
B-E-A-T-Beat-em-Beat-em
B-E-A-T-Beat-em-Beat-em
Beeeeeeeeeeeee-eat-em!!!!!

A Brockagh Book
www.liffeyrivers.com